MURDER IN THE ALPS

HIGH SOCIETY LADY DETECTIVE
BOOK EIGHT

SARA ROSETT

MURDER IN THE ALPS

A 1920s Historical Mystery

Book Eight in the High Society Lady Detective series

Published by McGuffin Ink

Hardcover ISBN: 978-1-950054-74-9

Paperback ISBN: 978-1-950054-73-2

Audiobook ISBN: 978-1-950054-76-3

Large Print ISBN: 978-1-950054-75-6

Copyright © 2023 by Sara Rosett

Book cover design by ebooklaunch.com

Editing: Historical Editorial

Map illustration: BMR Williams

❀ Created with Vellum

A NOTE ABOUT THE POLICE
FORCE IN SWITZERLAND

Thanks to Sandra Nay of the Graubünden State Archives and Anita Senti, Head of Communications of the Cantonal Police, for researching and sharing the details of the structure of the police force in St. Moritz in the 1920s.

I have created a fictional police station and the characters of the officers described in this book.

Any differences in the structure of the police force or the investigation of crime from real life are intentional for the sake of the fictional plot. If there are any mistakes, they are my own.

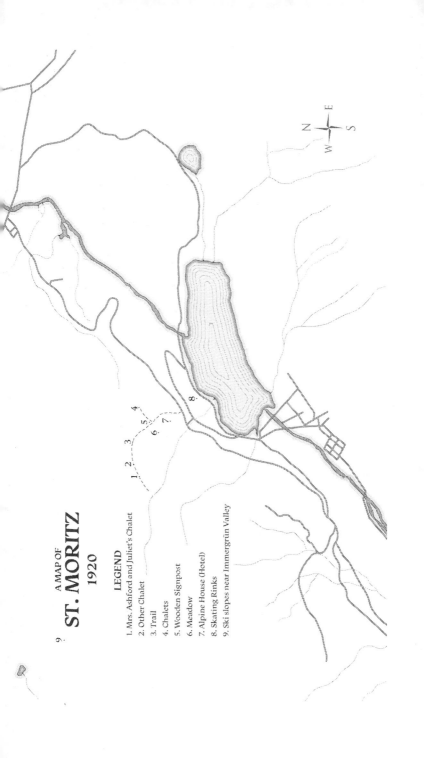

A MAP OF
ST. MORITZ
1920

LEGEND

1. Mrs. Ashford and Juliet's Chalet
2. Other Chalet
3. Trail
4. Chalets
5. Wooden Signpost
6. Meadow
7. Alpine House (Hotel)
8. Skating Rinks
9. Ski slopes near Immergrün Valley

CHAPTER 1

FEBRUARY 1924

*I*s there any more satisfactory feeling than correctly identifying the murderer?

I turned the last page of the book and closed it, feeling a bit smug because I'd worked out who did it before the denouement. I came back to my surroundings, aware of the quiet that permeated the train. No footfalls in the corridor or muted chatter filtered through the door to my compartment as it had earlier in the evening when I settled down after dinner with my mystery novel. The only sounds now were the steady thrum of the train's wheels and the occasional creak of the carriages as we swished through a turn on our way to the Alps.

I pushed back the blankets and emerged from the warm cocoon of my berth. The upper bunk was unoccupied, so I'd had the compartment to myself, a luxury that I'd never experienced. In fact, I was rather gobsmacked that I was actually traveling on the Engadine Express, an opulent train on par with some of the grandest trains in the world, like the Orient Express and le Train Bleu. When Jasper invited me on this jaunt, I'd been enormously satisfied that I'd been able to pay for my fare myself, especially considering that less than a year ago I'd had so little money I could only afford two-penny buns. Thank goodness I'd been able to pay my own way. I couldn't have accompanied Jasper otherwise. I might be a modern young lady, one of the new working girls, but I certainly couldn't let Jasper buy my ticket. That just wasn't the done thing—at least not for proper young ladies.

I picked up my sponge bag, creamed my face, and brushed my teeth at the small sink fitted into the corner of my compartment, then I shrugged into my dressing gown. I checked my watch that I'd placed on the little wooden table at my bedside. I'd wound it when I took it off earlier in the evening. When I held it to my ear, it was still ticking steadily, a tiny counterpoint to the rhythmic turn of the train wheels. I put it under the lamp on the table, the only light I'd had the attendant leave on in my compartment. Nearly half past one. Goodness, I had been swept up in the book. At least I wouldn't have to wait for the loo at the end of the carriage.

The door to my compartment didn't open smoothly. It had stuck earlier when I left for dinner, and I didn't want to yank it open with a bang that would wake my neighbors, so I eased it open.

". . . we must take advantage while we're in St. Moritz . . . never have an opportunity . . . again." I froze as the words carried down the hallway only a whisper above the noise of the train. Someone was standing out of my view. The voice was low and furtive. I didn't want to interrupt, so I gripped the door handle, intending to carefully close the door and wait a few minutes before leaving my compartment, but a second voice, also lowered, answered. Tension threaded through the intermittent words that filtered in through the noise of the train.

"Are . . . wise? What about the body? How . . . get rid . . . frozen ground . . . difficult."

I didn't dare move. A tiny squeak would give my presence away, and I knew instantly in that instinctive way that one knows something in one's very soul that I didn't want the two people in the passage to know I'd overheard them.

"Simple," the first person replied. ". . . all worked out. We don't have long before the attendant returns . . . tell you more . . ." They were moving away from me toward the other end of the carriage—thank goodness—their conversation fading. A door opened. Was it another door in *this* carriage? I strained to hear more, hoping they'd moved on to the next carriage, but above the steady pulse of the wheels I heard a second click as a door closed.

I rested my forehead against the shiny veneer of the doorframe. "Oh my."

The next morning, Jasper took the seat opposite me at the linen-covered table in the dining car. "Good morning, old bean." He motioned to the book I'd put beside my plate. "I take it you finished your mystery?"

"I stayed up far too late, and now I rather wish I

hadn't." I pushed *Murder on the Links* across the table to him. "I thought you might want to have a go at it as well."

He picked up the menu card. "Never regret reading into the wee hours, that's my motto. It sounds like this was an excellent read, if you couldn't put it down."

"The story wasn't the only thing that kept me up."

Jasper removed his monocle from his eye and put down the card. "Not feeling well?" He nodded at my untouched cup of hot cocoa and my plate with a single golden roll on it. Despite the melting Swiss butter, I'd only managed one bite of the crispy bread.

"I don't have much of an appetite."

"I'm sorry to hear that."

I waited until the waiter had poured Jasper a cup of coffee and left a fresh basket of rolls, then I leaned forward and whispered, "I overheard someone planning a murder."

Jasper choked on his coffee and dabbed his chin with his napkin. "Mur—?" Heads turned at his incredulous tone. He lowered his voice. "Murder? Are you sure?"

"Fairly certain. I've thought of nothing else since half past one last night and don't know what else they could have been discussing."

"They?"

"Yes, two people." I described how I'd come to over-hear the voices in the passageway outside my compart-ment, then said, "One person said they had to take advantage of the situation while they were in St. Moritz. I didn't see them, and they kept their voices down, but I could still hear their conversation. Anyway, after the first person said that about taking advantage of the situation, the other person didn't seem to agree and said, '*What about the body?*'"

Jasper broke a roll in half. "That conversation doesn't necessarily mean murder." He focused on spreading butter across the warm crinkles of the bread's interior. "Perhaps all these recent—um—incidents, shall we call them, which have been of the rather deadly variety, have impacted your perception a tiny bit? The people could have been talking about a body of water or a body of work—paintings, books, something along those lines."

I couldn't be cross with Jasper because when he raised his gaze to meet mine, there was nothing but concern in his expression. "I wish that were the case—I really do. And I'll admit that I couldn't hear every word, but I do know that the second person went on to say something about getting rid of it. I definitely caught the words *frozen ground* and *difficult.*"

Jasper put down his knife. "I say, that does sound rather ominous."

"I agree. I can't put any other interpretation on it."

"No, you're right, old bean. Sorry to doubt you. You have no idea who it could've been? No hint of an accent or distinctive way of speaking? Gravelly? High-pitched? Nasal?"

"No, not at the low volume they were speaking. I couldn't distinguish much. One person's voice was higher pitched and the other's was lower, which makes me think it was a man and a woman." I glanced around the dining car, which was packed with passengers. Sunlight flashed on the silver teapots and gleamed on the polished mahogany walls. The quiet clink of china teacups being

9

replaced in saucers and the low murmur of polite conversation permeated the atmosphere.

"It seems so unlikely, but as you said, after recent events I've learned not to be deceived by appearances."

Jasper put down his roll and looked around discreetly. "And it seems someone on this train has murderous intentions."

✦

CHAPTER 2

"*I* feel the appropriate thing to do is inform someone in authority, but I'm not sure who that would be on the train," I said. "I suppose once we reach St. Moritz, I should report it to the police. But other than the fact that I heard two doors close, which indicates both people were in the same carriage as we were, I can't tell them much more than that."

I scanned the occupants of the dining car. I hadn't paid that much attention to the other passengers on the train, but I couldn't help but study them now, wondering if two of them had been in the passageway last night. A woman in her mid-forties was seated at the table directly across the aisle from us. I recognized her. I'd seen her picture in the paper when I was a child. She was Amy Ashford, a lady mountaineer who had climbed many of the peaks in the Alps.

The article had made quite an impression on me. At the time, it hadn't occurred to me that ladies could do the sort of thing she was doing. Mountain climbing was considered mostly a manly sport, but her verve and energy came through in the article. When the interviewer asked why a lady like herself wanted to climb the peaks, she had replied, "Why not? Why shouldn't ladies participate in the sport? The mountains aren't only the province of men." The whole article had resonated with me, and I remembered it even now.

Jasper noticed the direction of my gaze, and I asked, "Do you recognize her?"

"Of course. It's Mrs. Ashford, the famous mountaineer."

"It's hard to believe she could have anything to do with what I overheard last night."

Mrs. Ashford wore a green tweed travel suit with a matching felt Tyrolean hat accented with a red feather. Although her brown hair was bobbed, there was something about the style of her clothes—the longer hemline that came down to the ankles—and her upright posture that indicated she had more in common with the Victorians than anything from the new century.

The waiter refilled Mrs. Ashford's coffee, and she gave him a smile, which exposed a crooked-tooth grin.

A trill of laughter rang out from another table of four people breakfasting together. Mrs. Ashford turned in that direction, and her smile vanished. Disapproval flashed across her face as she watched the group.

A young couple sat on one side of the table. The woman was probably in her mid-twenties, with shiny golden hair curling out from under the brim of her hat, which matched her pale pink travel suit. Like Mrs. Ashford, her hat was in the Tyrolean style, but while Mrs. Ashford looked as if she'd picked hers up at an Alpine shop in a local village, I was sure that the fair-haired young woman across the dining car had purchased hers in Paris. It had that extra flair that only an expert milliner could achieve.

The blonde was a beauty, with a creamy complexion, cherry-red lips, eyebrows plucked to a perfect arch, and pale blue eyes. Her companion sat with his arm draped casually across the back of her chair. He held a cigarette in his other hand and wafted smoke rings into the air above his wiry dark brown hair. He was in casual attire of the type the Prince of Wales had made popular, a Fair Isle V-neck jumper over a shirt. With his square-jawed face and broad-shouldered build, he looked as if he were ready to pose for a Thomas Cook & Son travel poster—the hardy hiker with a length of rope looped over his shoulder as he stood, legs planted on a rock, surveying a mountain range.

Two younger men sat across the table from the couple, both with a thatch of fair hair and freckles. They were so similar-looking I wondered if they were brothers. Their expressions were identical. Both were full of wide-eyed admiration as they looked at the man across the table.

"Mrs. Ashford doesn't look pleased with the party of four. Do you know them?" I asked as I took a sip of my cocoa.

Jasper casually turned and surveyed the dining car behind him then turned back. "The two young chaps on one side of the table are in a compartment near mine. I met them yesterday. They're on the way to St. Moritz to ice climb. They're training with the man across the table from them, Mr. Lavington. Apparently, Mr. Lavington is quite the expert in ice-climbing and mountaineering in general. I gathered that both of the younger men are rather in awe of him. One is named Blinkhorn—the one seated on the aisle, I think. They do resemble each other, don't they? They might be twins, but the last names are different. The other's name is . . . let me think. Oh yes, Ignatius Hale. If all goes well here, the three will make an assault on Everest in the future."

"Do you know the young woman?"

"Mr. Lavington's wife, Emmaline. I haven't talked with her on the train, but I remember when she was a deb."

"I'm sure you did your duty and danced with her."

"Yes, I did. She was a sensation. Several lads were head over heels for her."

"I can see why. She's very pretty. She has the look of the fragile china doll."

"On the exterior, certainly, but at the core, she's rather willful and spoiled."

I raised my eyebrows. "Jasper! That's not like you to say something so critical."

"The truth is often unpleasant. If you spend any time in her company, I'm sure you'll agree. She was a guest at a shooting party I attended last year in Scotland. Emmaline and several other ladies went out on the moors with us one day. Nothing, absolutely nothing, was enjoyable to her, and she made sure everyone knew it. The weather, the food, the views, her shoes. Nothing was to her liking. She even sent a servant back to the house to bring her a fresh pair of shoes."

"So no stiff upper lip?"

"Decidedly not."

"I wonder which person it is that Mrs. Ashford disapproves of. She still has a scowl on her face when she glances back at them."

"Perhaps it's simply because they're making so much noise."

Emmaline's voice carried through the air. "No more talk of ropes and merits of this over that one. And let's stop with the never-ending debate about portable oxygen. You boys are too, too boring. Tell me, what else do you intend to do in St. Moritz besides climb?" She waited a beat, then said, "Come on, there must be *something*."

Her husband, in an urbane drawl, said, "Darling, leave them alone. Climbing is the reason they're going to St. Moritz. Just like you're going for the shops."

She patted him on the cheek. "And you'll frown and grumble at the price tags as you always do." She looked back across the table to the young men. "Ben is rather keen on budgets and sticking to them. So tiresome of him."

Another couple entered the dining car. The woman wore an austere navy suit and had black curls and pale skin. Her companion had thinning ginger hair, a ruddy complexion, and the bulky build of a man who had once been fit but was now going soft around the middle. Unlike the other men in the carriage, who wore tweeds or sporty jumpers and jackets, he had on a pinstriped suit with a gold chain across his vest. He followed the waiter with a lumbering gait to a table, but the woman broke off and darted across the carriage, calling, "Emmaline!"

I could see the expression on Mrs. Lavington's face when her name was called. Her eyes widened and the corners of her lips flattened into a look that could only be irritation. She sent a covert glance toward her husband before she reached for her handbag. The dark-haired woman arrived at the table, and the three men stood. Mrs.

Lavington remained seated and removed a cigarette from a case before looking up.

The brunette said, "I thought we might not see you until we got to St. Moritz." She flapped her hand at the men. "Oh, do sit down. I'm only stopped for a moment to say hello." She had small, close-set eyes with stubby eyelashes and narrow lips. Her clothes were of the best quality. She had forgone the Tyrolean hat and wore a cloche with an unusual disk-like brim that dipped over one eye. It wasn't a style I'd seen before, and it rivaled Mrs. Lavington's hat for its exquisite panache. I could hear my stepmother Sonia's voice declaring that, despite her finery, the brunette couldn't hold a candle to her chic friend.

The men resumed their seats, and Mrs. Lavington said, "I had no idea you'd be in St. Moritz, Hattie."

Jasper and I couldn't help but overhear the conversation. Only one table separated us from the group.

The dark-haired woman said, "Robbie and I are having a bit of a holiday. It's hard to wrest him away from the bank, but I managed it. A friend's mother said you were traveling here as well, which is absolutely perfect. We have so *much* to talk about."

The last sentence had a slightly barbed quality to it. Jasper picked up on the tone and raised an eyebrow.

I said, sotto voce, "Yes, there's something going on there."

Mrs. Lavington bent toward the flame of the lighter her husband held out. "If we bump into each other, we'll have to do that. St. Moritz is rather congested at this time of year."

"Oh, don't worry. I'll be in touch." Her words had the ring of a challenge about them.

I studied the brunette as she strode down the aisle to the table where the man—her husband?—held a chair for her. I picked up my cocoa. It was barely warm now, so I put it down again, my attention still on the Lavingtons' table. "It looks like the group of four is breaking up."

The Lavingtons and the two young men pushed back their chairs. Mrs. Ashford noticed the movement, and she quickly departed the dining car.

Mrs. Lavington was digging around in her handbag as she walked by our table. "Oh, bother. I left my cigarette case at the table. No, don't wait for me," she said to her husband. "I'll only be a moment."

She went back to the table, and the three men left the dining car. As she retraced her steps to leave, her glance fell on Jasper, and she paused. "Jasper Rimington! It's been ages since I've seen you. How are you?"

Jasper stood. "Very well, thank you. And you?"

"I'm well. Quite well. Are you on your way to St. Moritz?"

"I am. I'm looking forward to a few days in the mountains."

"We are too. How wonderful." Her gaze strayed to me. "And is this Miss Ravenna?" A hint of mischief laced through the words. She was referring to a famous London stage actress whose name had often been linked with Jasper's in the gossip columns.

"Oh no. Let me introduce you," Jasper said, his easy manner unfazed. "This is Miss Olive Belgrave. Olive, this is Mrs. Lavington."

"How do you do?" I asked, but she didn't give the expected reply.

When she heard my name, a look of delight spread across her face. "Olive Belgrave, the lady detective! Why, this is too, too perfect. I must speak with you." She looked quickly at the door where her husband and the two young climbers had exited the dining car. "Privately."

CHAPTER 3

*B*efore I could reply to Mrs. Lavington, Jasper put some coins on the table and picked up the novel as he said, "I have packing to do before we arrive, so I'll leave you two ladies. Goodbye, Mrs. Lavington. Olive, I'll arrange for porters for our luggage."

"Won't you join me?" I gestured to the seat across the table that Jasper had vacated.

"No, not here. What number is your compartment?"

"Six."

"Brilliant. I'll leave first and meet you there." She dashed out the door.

I contemplated my untouched roll and cold cocoa, then pushed back my chair.

I went to my compartment and checked to make sure I hadn't missed any of my belongings when I packed this morning before breakfast. Seconds later a staccato rapping sounded. It had to be Mrs. Lavington. The attendant always tapped and waited politely, but this person knocked again when I didn't open the door immediately.

"Coming." I put my handbag with my luggage, glad ▮▮▮ that my compartment was tidy.

Mrs. Lavington crossed the threshold and quickly pulled the door from my hand to close it, shoving it over the point where it stuck. "There." She turned back to me, her cheeks as pink as her travel suit. "I can't tell you how thrilled I am that you're on this train. You're exactly the person I need. I'll have nothing to do with those scruffy little private detective men, but you're different. You're a lady. I'm sure you'll understand."

Without waiting for an invitation, she sat down on the berth. I took a seat beside her. "How can I help?"

She squared her shoulders as if she were preparing for an unpleasant task. Despite the fact that we were alone in the compartment with the door securely shut, she dropped her voice. "I'm being blackmailed." She sat back and waited for my reaction. I kept my face blank, as if this were the sort of conversation I had after breakfast each morning.

My lack of reaction must have irritated her because she said, "I need you to make it stop," in a way that suggested I was rather slow.

I took a moment to formulate an answer. "I see. Well, stopping a blackmailer is often rather difficult. Why don't you tell me the details?"

She held her petit-point handbag in her lap, and her grip tightened on its jade clasp. "I received another letter —a demand, I should say—last night from this awful person, so it must be someone on this train. Surely you can figure out who's sending me those awful letters."

"You said you received *another* letter? Why don't we start at the beginning? When did you receive the first one?" I opened my travel case and took out a notepad, but Mrs. Lavington gave me a horrified look and flicked her fingers. "Put that away. Nothing in writing. I can't risk it. If you lose your notebook and my details are in there, that would be ghastly. Absolutely ghastly. You must promise not to tell anyone else about this."

"I won't talk about this to anyone else." I put the notebook down and turned back to her. "Your husband doesn't know?"

"No, of course not. And it's becoming more and more difficult to keep it from him. He asked about the note last night. Fortunately, I managed to put him off with a story about a delayed letter from a cousin. He had no interest in *that*."

I glanced at her handbag. After her preemptory wave and request that I banish my notebook, she'd again gripped its frame. "Do you have the note with you?"

"No! I burned it."

I kept my expression neutral, but I wished she'd kept the note instead of destroying it. "Well, what did it look like? Tell me everything you can about it."

"It was on white paper, and the envelope was white as well. That's all I remember. I hate those horrid letters, and I wanted it out of my sight as soon as possible. I got rid of it at the first opportunity."

"I understand. A note of that sort would be very distressing. Perhaps I can help you recall a few more details. What sort of paper was it? Heavy and thick or light and flimsy?"

A frown creased Mrs. Lavington's forehead. "Medium weight, I suppose."

"Letterhead?"

"No, just plain white paper, as I said."

Impatience tinged her reply, but I pressed on. "And the handwriting?"

"It was typed. Why all these useless questions? Obviously, the person took care to make sure there was nothing identifiable about it. You should be talking to the porter who brought me the note."

"All in good time. Only a few more questions. Small details can be quite revealing. First, what did the note say?"

"I was to obtain ten pounds," she said in a scandalized tone, which surprised me. Looking at her clothing and knowing that she was on her way to St. Moritz, I would have thought ten pounds would be a small sum to her.

"And that was all?" I asked. "Nothing else? No directions on what to do with the money?"

"No, just that I'm *to await further instructions*." She sniffed with disapproval. "As if I'm an errand boy at someone's beck and call."

I refrained from pointing out that her status was remarkably similar to an errand boy. Instead, I said, "And this has happened before?"

"Yes, several times. But in the past, the amount had only been five pounds and the"—she twisted her crimson lips into a grimace—"instructions on how to deliver the money were included in the letter."

"And what were the delivery instructions when it happened previously?"

"I don't see why it matters." She gave an impatient shake of her head. Her golden curls trembled against the ivory skin of her cheeks. "That's in the past. All that matters is what's happening *now*."

"Nevertheless, knowing the history might give us some insight into how you'll be asked to deliver the money."

Her expression showed that she didn't agree, but she must have decided to humor me because she drew in a deep breath, which managed to convey that she found me extremely exasperating. "Very well, I'll detail it for you, but it won't help you now."

"Why don't you let me be the judge of that?"

"Fine." She launched into an explanation, the cadence of her words quick.

CHAPTER 4

"In the past," Mrs. Lavington said with a certain amount of bite to her words, "the instructions in the notes were to put the money in an envelope, then put the envelope in a newspaper, which had been folded in half. I was to take it to St. James's Park and sit on a certain bench for a few moments. At precisely noon, I was to leave it on the bench and walk away without looking back. See, as I said, that's no help at all when you're on a train. The instructions can't be the same."

I chose to ignore her last comments. "And did you?"

She frowned. "Follow the instructions? Well, yes."

"No, I meant, did you look back?"

"Of course I looked back," she said witheringly, then her expression turned sulky. "And each time a young boy ran over, snatched up the newspaper, and ran off." She smoothed out a fold in her pink skirt, concentrating on adjusting the luxurious fabric. "Before you ask, it was a different boy each time—one was scrawny with a fringe of dark hair. The next time the boy was taller and had lighter hair. I always followed the boys, but they were too fast for me. I never managed to catch them before they disappeared into the crowds."

"You said *each* time. How many times has this happened?"

"In London? Several, I'm sorry to say."

I pushed down my irritation with her and wondered why she was so reluctant to discuss the details. But then, blackmail isn't something one wishes to expound on. I kept my tone pleasant as I asked, "How often did it happen? Every month?"

"Oh no. I don't know the exact dates, but I do remember I received one letter around Christmas. Incredibly inconvenient when one is trying to plan for gifts and travel. And then there was another in spring. It was around April, I suppose. And then the last one before this one came in the summer. I do know the exact day that one arrived, Midsummer's Eve. We'd been invited to a party, and I was so distraught I couldn't enjoy myself that night."

"But nothing in the autumn?"

"No. I thought the person had become bored with their tedious little game or that they'd been satisfied."

"Blackmailers are rarely satisfied. All the notes that you received were the same? Typed on white paper?"

"Yes." She opened her purse and took out her lighter and a cigarette. "You don't mind if I smoke, do you?"

"Yes, in fact, I do. Cigarette smoke and I don't agree. I'm allergic," I said, but by the time I'd finished speaking, she'd already lit up.

Mrs. Lavington shifted her knees so she was facing the opposite direction. "I'll blow it away from you." She demonstrated by exhaling over her shoulder into the corner of the compartment, but wisps of the acrid smell drifted up the wall and then floated toward me.

The muscles in my cheeks strained as I worked to keep the smile on my face. "I'd really prefer you put it out. It's such a small area."

"Nonsense. It'll be fine." With the cigarette clamped between her first two gloved fingers, she made little twitches with her other fingers, indicating I should lower the window. "Just open it a bit. I'll stand over there, and you'll never notice."

I was beginning to wonder if I really wanted Mrs. Lavington as a client. But my days of scraping to pay the bills and buy food weren't that far behind me, so I held my breath and lowered the window a few inches. Then I stepped across to the other side of the compartment by the door. "So going back to the blackmail notes . . . was there anything distinctive about the typing? Any of the letters smudged or not aligned? Some more faded than others?"

"I don't know." She stood and blew out a long stream of smoke. Some of it went out the window, but tendrils of it curled up to the ceiling and crawled my way. I dropped my gaze back to Mrs. Lavington, who said, "As soon as I saw what the letters were, I burned them. I didn't spend time examining them."

"That's a pity because it might have given us some more information."

She swayed with the movement of the train, her shoulders shifting back and forth slightly. "Like what?"

"Typed pages can often be matched to the machine they were produced on. If we could find the typewriter—"

27

"Well, that's not a possibility. As I said, I don't have any of the letters." The floor of the compartment shifted as the train traveled around a curve and into a tunnel, briefly plunging us into darkness.

A few moments later we came out the other side, and Mrs. Lavington leaned against the wall of the compartment. She crossed her arms but kept her hand with the cigarette angled away from her body. "So what can you do about it? How soon can you find out which awful person on this train is doing this and put a stop to it?"

I squashed a sigh at her naïveté. "As I said, once you've paid a blackmailer, it's extremely difficult to put an end to it. There's really only two ways it goes. Either you remove the person's leverage—"

She was about to take a drag but paused with the cigarette by her lips. "What do you mean?"

"You remove whatever hold they have over you. For instance, if you're having an affair, you tell your husband."

Her crimson lips parted in a laugh. "I assure you, that's not the trouble. I'd never be so stupid as to do that. Once Ben climbs Mt. Everest, everyone will know his name. There will be the possibility of a knighthood in the future, I'm sure."

"Well, whatever the blackmailer is holding over you, you take the initiative and you reveal it. Once the secret is out, the blackmailer has no power over you."

"That's not going to happen," she said sharply. She switched her attention to the view of rocky crags and evergreens layered with snow. "It's gone on too long. I couldn't do it now. I'd look like a fool. What's the other way things can go?"

"You catch the blackmailer and expose him—or her."

"Then that's what it will have to be."

"All right. You'll need to keep me informed and let me know when you receive the next instructions with the details on how to deliver the money." I'd not ever caught a blackmailer in the act, but it seemed the logical way to go about discovering the culprit.

She whirled around. "No. That's not what I want *at all*. You will speak to the porter and find out who handed over that envelope to him."

"I could do that, but the blackmailer may have had a second party hand off the envelope."

"Well then, follow the trail back." She made a circular motion with the cigarette, indicating I should get moving. I breathed shallowly as the smoke drifted lazily toward me. I tried to ignore the prickly sensation in the back of my throat. If my breathing became wheezy, all I had to do was open the door and step into the corridor for fresh air.

"It may not be that simple," I warned her. "The most efficient thing to do is to watch and see who picks up the money you deliver—keep an eye out discreetly, of course. Can you think of anyone who would do this? Do you have any connections with anyone on the train?"

"I know the boys my husband is training, but I only met them a few weeks ago. They're just puppies. They have no reason to do anything like this. Hattie and her husband, Rob, are on the train." Her lids narrowed into slits as she drew on the cigarette again. "It could be her," she said as she exhaled smoke.

"Anyone else?"

"There have been a few other familiar faces—like Mr. Rimington—but no one I know intimately."

"Then it definitely will be most efficient to see who picks up the money."

A gust of wind surged through the window, tugging at the feather on her hat and ruffling her curls. She stepped away from the window. "But that's not what I'm hiring you to do." She continued in the tone one would use to explain something to a child. "I want you to speak to everyone on the train. We still have time before we arrive in St. Moritz. Do it now. You'll have to hurry because you've spent so long on worrying over what happened in the past." When I didn't move, her perfectly plucked eyebrows arched up. "What are you waiting for? Get going. Time is short." She turned to the mirror over the sink and checked the angle of her hat while still holding the cigarette.

I shook my head. "I'm sorry, but I can't take your case." No amount of money was worth working with someone who was so set on her own path that she wouldn't even consider another approach.

"What?" She stared at my reflection for a moment, then turned to face me. "What's your usual fee? Whatever it is, I'll double it."

CHAPTER 5

"I'm afraid money isn't the issue," I said to Mrs. Lavington as the floor of the compartment shifted again with the movement of the train. "We have a difference of opinion about how the case should be handled. I don't think I would be able to meet your expectations. It's best you find someone who agrees with your approach." It was always good to have another client lined up, and I was curious if the blackmail was connected to the conversation I'd overheard last night; but I wasn't about to put myself in a situation where Mrs. Lavington treated me like a lapdog who should jump at her command. I might have done that a few months ago, but my bank account was healthy enough that I could pass this case up.

I opened the door, tugging it past the point where it stuck, and let in a stream of clear air. I took a deep breath of it, then stepped back to allow her room to leave.

She blew a stream of smoke out the window, gazing at me from the corner of her eye. "You're a very foolish woman. I would have paid you well." She tossed her cigarette out the window, jerked up her handbag from where she'd laid it on the berth, and marched to the door. As she crossed the threshold into the corridor, she collided with a stylish woman with auburn hair who was carrying some papers. Mrs. Lavington jerked backward and gave the woman a curt greeting. "Juliet."

During the near collision, the woman had lost her grip on some of the papers, and now she tucked them back into alignment. "Mrs. Lavington." She gestured for Mrs. Lavington to precede her down the corridor. They didn't exchange any more words, but tension charged their exchange.

The woman named Juliet paused, giving Mrs. Lavington time to stride away, then she gave me a small nod of acknowledgment before continuing down the corridor. A newspaper lay on the floor where she'd stood. I called out, "Excuse me, you dropped your paper."

I picked it up and held it out. She'd circled back, but then said, "Oh, thank you, but I'm done with that."

It was a London paper. "If you don't mind, I'll keep it. My friend draws a cartoon, and I've missed a few installments while traveling."

"Keep it, by all means." She hesitated, then asked, "It's not Minerva Blythe, is it?"

"Yes, it is."

"I simply adore her cartoons. Such fun! And underneath the froth, there's some very adroit social commentary."

"I agree."

The woman stuck out her hand. "I'm Juliet Lenox."

"Pleased to meet you. Olive Belgrave."

"I gather you're on your way to St. Moritz?" When I nodded, she continued. "So you must enjoy winter sports?"

"Well, I brought my ice skates, but that's the extent of my winter sporting abilities."

"Then you're welcome to join our group." She took a business card from her pocket and handed it to me.

It read, *Ladies' Winter Sporting Association* and had her name below it.

"I'm the secretary of the association," Juliet said. "Our goal is to promote ladies' winter sports. The men have their skiing and are rumbling on about making the toboggan run for men only. Mrs. Ashford—the mountaineer, you know—is the real impetus behind the organization, but I wholeheartedly agree that women should have their own winter sports organization. And Lady Mulvern has just joined the board."

"Did you say Lady *Mulvern?*" I knew Lady Mulvern, and she didn't seem like the sporty type—of any season, either summer or winter.

"Yes, she visited St. Moritz a few weeks ago. Lady Foyle invited her to join the committee. She's—Lady Foyle, I mean—is on the committee with Mrs. Ashford. Lady Mulvern was a smashing success as a skier. Absolutely adored it! Some people have a natural talent for it. She was quite chuffed at having something to do while her husband was tobogganing."

"I imagine so."

"And Lady Mulvern has the most precious little cat. I told Lady Foyle that the cat should be our mascot. Lady Mulvern was completely taken with the idea. However, Lady Foyle was rather doubtful." Juliet straightened the papers in her arms again. "With Lady Mulvern on the board, I think we're poised for growth. Lady Foyle and Mrs. Ashford have had the idea for the association for years, but with the war, well, it wasn't possible."

She paused, and we both fell silent for a moment. Sporting activities had been the last thing on anyone's mind during the war. "Once the war ended, Lady Foyle returned to the idea. I've spent quite a bit of time this last year shuttling back and forth between here and London to get the organization off the ground. At the moment, we're focused on skating and skiing. We're having a ladies' ski race soon. You're welcome to participate."

"Perhaps I should see if I can stand up on skis before I participate in a race." My curiosity got the better of me, and I asked, "And the woman who nearly ran you down, is she a member as well?"

"Emmaline?" Juliet's tone indicated my question was incredibly absurd. "No. Emmaline has no interest in any type of athletic pursuit. Are you a friend of hers?"

"I met her this morning."

"Well, Emmaline Lavington has a delicate constitution." Juliet flared an eyebrow. "At least she insists she does. She was ill as a child."

"So you've known her a long while?"

"Yes, but I met her after her childhood sickness. I'm not sure if she ever was as frightfully ill as she says."

I made a noncommittal noise. The conversation was confirmation for me that I'd made the right decision in not working for Mrs. Lavington. Perhaps it had slipped Mrs. Lavington's mind that Juliet Lenox was on the train. Or Mrs. Lavington had deliberately lied to me. Either way, I was glad I didn't have to sort it out.

"Well, I hope to see you once we arrive in St. Moritz," Juliet said. "Enjoy your paper."

The train ran into the station, and I put the paper in my luggage and went to meet Jasper on the platform. The air was frosty, and my breath made little white clouds, but the day was clear and sunny. The platform had been cleared of snow. It was piled up in drifts, rounded hillocks at least six feet high, glistening in the sun. I made my way across little rivulets of water tracing away from the piles of snow. They crisscrossed the surface, their wiggly lines seeming to represent rivers on a giant relief map that was the surface of the platform.

Jasper caught sight of me. He waved from his position by a porter, who was stacking our luggage on a trolley.

When I walked up to him, he asked, "Do you have news after your chat with Mrs. Lavington? Will you be pursuing business as well as pleasure in the Alps?"

"No, I'm not taking on Mrs. Lavington as a client."

Jasper had looked back to check the progress of the porter, but at my words he swiveled back to me and leaned forward slightly. "You aren't?"

"We had differing views on how to approach her problem. I don't believe I can produce the results that she expects."

Jasper gave me a small smile. "Few people do meet her expectations. I must say, I think you've made a wise choice, old bean." He reached into his coat and took out a sheet of paper. "For you, compliments of the train attendant."

I opened it and found a diagram of the train carriage, each compartment labeled with the names of the occupants. "I thought it would be a good idea for you to have the names, in case you speak to the police."

"Why, Jasper, thank you. How did you get this from the train attendant?"

"I simply had a little chat with the fellow and asked him if he could jot down the names for me. He was most obliging."

I tilted my head. "Did you pay him?"

"No. I hinted I had a wager that a certain person was staying in a certain compartment, and he could help me win the bet in exchange for a pack of cigarettes."

I refolded the paper and ran my gloved fingers along the crease. "I've been wavering on whether or not I should report what I heard. Since I can't describe who it was, perhaps I shouldn't say anything at all. My information is rather sketchy. And even if I hand over this list of names, I doubt the police will investigate each one. I'm sure they have better things to do than pursue such a vague complaint."

"Well, at least a dead body didn't turn up on the train this morning. For that, I'm immensely grateful. That would have slowed up my tobogganing, don't you know, not to mention interfering with the other reason for this trip."

"Looking forward to getting down to work, are you?"

"Quite. It's time to knock the dust off the old brain box. And speaking of that," Jasper raised his hand and waved, "there's Bebe."

CHAPTER 6

*M*iss Bebe Ravenna's willowy figure was completely engulfed in a calf-length mink coat. A hat in matching fur contrasted with her platinum bob. She raised a leather-gloved hand in an elegant gesture of acknowledgment and made her way across the platform. Jasper lifted his hat when she reached us. "Hello, Bebe."

"Hello, old thing. Good to see you, Jasper." She turned to me and shook my hand. "I'm delighted that we're able to meet again so soon after the holidays, Miss Belgrave."

"I am as well." The words were the appropriate social response, but I was truly glad to see Miss Ravenna. I could admit to myself now, as I looked back over the last few months, that I'd been a tad jealous of Miss Ravenna—well, perhaps more than a tad. Miss Ravenna was a beauty, a talented actress on stage and in the cinema, and she had kept popping up in Jasper's company, which the newspaper photographers made sure to document. If Jasper accompanied Miss Ravenna to a party or took her to dinner, the pictures had been in the paper the next day, which could really put a girl off her breakfast. But I'd finally met Miss Ravenna in person at Christmastime and found her to be warm and friendly. I'd also learned that there was a very good reason she was in Jasper's company so often—and it had nothing to do with romance, despite what the newspapers hinted.

Miss Ravenna said, "Fortunately, I was able to complete my errands in Germany rather quickly. It looks like I may be returning to England soon."

Jasper adjusted his wool scarf, tucking it under the lapels of his thick overcoat. "Is the stage calling? Have you received an excellent script?"

"No, I'll have a new role. However, it's not on the stage. I intend to produce a film."

"How exciting," I said.

"Capital idea," Jasper said approvingly.

"It's all down to Evert." She turned and motioned to a man who stood a few paces behind her. He was tall, with sharp-planed features, gold-brown hair, and a reserved manner.

Bebe glued her arm to his and pulled him into our little group. "Evert, this is Jasper Rimington and Olive Belgrave, the two I've been telling you about. This is Evert Vandenberg. He's such a dear. Perhaps you've heard of him? He's originally from Sweden, and he's the most amazing director. He started with plays, and he's marvelous with those as well, but now he works in the German cinema. He's convinced me that I should produce a film."

Miss Ravenna was quite tall, but Mr. Vandenberg was a head taller than her, and she had to tilt her head up as she turned to smile at him in a way that would have been worthy of the ending credits of a romance movie. Their gaze locked, and Mr. Vandenberg said, "It's only fitting. Bebe knows exactly what it takes to get a film—a good film—made. After all, Mary Pickford has her own studio. Why not Bebe?" His perfect, careful enunciation and a faint trace of an accent that flittered through his words were the only hints that English wasn't his native language.

Miss Ravenna's laughter trilled through the crisp air. "Let me get one film made, darling, before I set my sights on a whole studio."

Mr. Vandenberg moved his shoulder and twitched his hand in a casual motion, as if to say that making a film wouldn't be that hard for her. "You will do it. I know it."

"Are you traveling on to England right away, or will you spend a few days here?" I asked, even though I already knew the answer. We had to keep up the fiction that our meeting hadn't been planned.

In fact, it was Miss Ravenna's telegram to Jasper that had initiated our trip. Besides her acting—and now it seemed producing would be added to her list of accomplishments—Bebe also had a sideline, helping further the security interests of Great Britain. Her position as a star gave her access to some of the places and people the government wanted to keep tabs on.

Her message had asked Jasper to meet her in St Moritz. I could only assume that Miss Ravenna had something that required Jasper's special skill of codebreaking. Of course, he'd been mum about the reason she'd requested he travel to Switzerland, which was understandable. I realized it was something he couldn't talk about. I didn't ask. But one could put two and two together.

"We'll stay for a few days, which will be marvelous." Miss Ravenna snuggled her arm closer to Mr. Vandenberg's. "I just love the air here—so clear, and it's actually quite warm when you're in the sun, despite being such a high altitude. And the views from the hotel terrace! It hasn't changed since I was here last year. It's truly an amazing place."

I felt someone hovering at the periphery of my vision and turned to find two young women. For a moment, I took them to be reporters because of the pens and paper they both held, but then I saw the starstruck look on their faces. Miss Ravenna had noticed them too. She disengaged her arm from Mr. Vandenberg. She greeted the girls, and the bolder of the two stepped forward.

"Miss Ravenna! It really is you! And you're even more gorgeous in person than you are on the screen. I've seen all your films. My favorite is *Meet You at Sunset*, but Joanie thinks *The Whole Nine Yards* was better. But—oh my goodness, I'm babbling. Anyway, we think you're the berries!"

Miss Ravenna smiled. "Thank you very much." She paused, but the two girls seemed to have been turned to stone like Lot's wife, so she asked, "Would you like me to sign something for you?"

"Oh yes," they chorused, breaking out of their trance. Miss Ravenna signed autographs for them. They retreated in cascades of fading giggles.

Miss Ravenna pulled her fur hat lower over her eyes and turned back to us. "Evert and I are just back from a trip to a dear little village, but our base is here at the Alpine House."

Jasper said, "Olive and I are staying there as well," as if the whole thing hadn't been planned for weeks.

"Smashing. We have a motor waiting," Miss Ravenna continued. "Perhaps you'd like to join us?" We accepted the offer, and the porters followed us to a perfectly polished Daimler, gleaming in the sunshine.

CHAPTER 7

St. Moritz was more a town than a village, nestled against a lake that curved through the long valley. It was quite a bit larger than the little Swiss community where I'd attended finishing school. Massive mountains surrounded the valley, their rocky peaks looking imposing even under a coating of snow. Layers of snow several inches deep also covered St. Moritz, blanketing the roofs of the luxurious hotels and shops and weighing down the boughs of evergreens.

Jasper, Miss Ravenna, Mr. Vandenberg, and I chatted about the train journey as the motor cruised along to the hotel. The town of St. Moritz proper clustered on the curved northwest side of the lake. The skating rinks, sled runs, hotels, and boutiques stair-stepped up the side of the mountain to the toboggan run above. The mountains across the lake weren't as developed. Dense ranks of evergreens, their branches heavy with snow, ran from a small strip of land at the edge of the lake upward until the trees gave way to the sheer snow-capped peaks.

Miss Ravenna asked, "What do you think, Miss Belgrave?"

"The beauty of this place—it's like something out of a fairy tale. One tends to forget how colossal the mountains are. It makes one feel quite small and insignificant indeed." The motor turned away from the lake, the engine revving as we climbed up a road that twisted through the town, and I shifted my attention away from the view to Miss Ravenna. "I suppose you're looking forward to skiing."

"Oh no. I don't ski."

"Really?" I was sure I'd seen photos of her last winter with skis on a mountain slope.

"You're thinking of the advert for skiwear from last season, I suppose? That's the magic of photography. I wore the clothes and posed on the mountain, but I snowshoed up there and back down. I'm quite accident prone. Not sporty at all, I'm afraid. I'm sure I'd be a disaster on skis." I found it hard to believe that Miss Ravenna was a disaster at anything. "Ah, we've arrived," she said as the motor rolled to a stop in front of the Alpine House.

The hotel's exterior was white stucco and stone. Its five stories were lined with wooden balconies carved with patterns of diamonds and other ornate shapes. The Alpine House was set on a rise, and it had been designed to take advantage of the geography. All the rooms located on the front of the hotel had a view of St. Moritz and the lake. The lowest area directly behind the hotel was a mix of open snow-covered ground and patchy trees. Pines dotted the higher elevations between open areas, which were wide swaths of snow. Higher up still, sled runs serpentined across the clear areas.

I had to shade my eyes against the glare of the sun on the slopes as I tilted my head back to see the mountain-tops. Towering steeply above the runs, the jagged white peaks dazzled against the clear blue sky.

The Alpine House Restaurant was connected to the hotel. Situated to the right of the main entrance, the restaurant's roof-top terrace was a popular attraction and already busy. Wisps of conversation and the clink of china drifted through the air along with the flap of the canvas umbrellas that shaded some of the tables. I'd had a wonderful afternoon lunch there on a day out with some chums a few years ago. I remembered the hotel had another terrace, one reserved for sunbathing, that stretched from the back of the hotel to the rising slope of the mountain.

I was surprised to see the Lavingtons exiting a taxi. I'd assumed they'd stay at one of the more luxurious hotels. The Alpine House hotel was a long-standing favorite in the area, but it was more cozy and had the atmosphere of a mountain lodge rather than a grand hotel.

As her husband paid the driver, Mrs. Lavington swept a fur stole around her neck and crossed to the hotel. The doorman, a middle-aged man, dressed in a top hat and a double-breasted overcoat with gold buttons, held the door open. Under his heavy brows, his gaze sharpened as Mrs. Lavington strode by him into the lobby. Mr. Lavington followed a second later and didn't seem to notice the doorman, but a plump middle-aged woman with light brown hair who held a small case halted and stared at the doorman, a look of shock on her face. I was close enough to hear her startled tone as she said, "Fredrick?"

The doorman's eyes widened for a second, and he seemed to gather himself to speak, but then Mrs. Lavington's sharp tones carried through the door the man still held open, "Etta! Don't dawdle."

The woman jumped as if someone had poked her in the back with an umbrella. She bolted across the threshold.

While the bellhops removed our luggage, Jasper ambled over. "Magnificent view, isn't it?"

"Incredible," I said, then felt the weight of Jasper's gaze travel from me to the doorman, whom I was still watching. "Something slightly odd caught my attention," I explained.

"I see. I thought for a moment there I might have competition for your affections."

I laughed. "From the doorman? He's at least in his forties."

"Such a scornful tone! Careful, I'm not that far behind him in years."

"Oh, pish. You know I'm not taken in by your monocle. You're only slightly older than me."

Jasper grinned at me as we went into the lobby. "Yes, I do tend to forget that you know my actual birthday. But why is the doorman looking daggers at Mrs. Lavington?" Jasper asked in a rhetorical tone. "Of course, she tends to put one's back up, so it's not *that* surprising."

A blast of heat engulfed me, and I pulled off my gloves. "But she didn't say a word to him. Didn't even glance at him."

The lobby was spacious, with wood-paneled walls and an ornate Jacobean-style paneled ceiling. A wide set of stairs with ornately carved banisters was directly across from the entrance, and doors to the right were open to the restaurant, where a few people were dining inside instead of on the terrace upstairs. Jasper and I paused to wait for Miss Ravenna and Mr. Vandenberg.

Mr. Lavington was at the front desk, while Mrs. Lavington stood just inside the door. Even though a large circular table topped with a vase of flowers separated us, her clear aristocratic tones were audible as she chatted with a woman who must have been a friend she'd crossed paths with. "Oh, darling, of course I had to come," Mrs. Lavington said. "I couldn't let Ben trot off on his own to Switzerland without me. Although I'm sure I won't know what to do with myself after a few days. Winter sports can be so very tedious after a day or so. I'll be frightfully bored. I'll have been through all the shops by then."

Miss Ravenna and Mr. Vandenberg joined us, a train of bellboys following them. As I unwound my wool scarf, Mrs. Lavington continued, "Isn't it disappointing that Kulm is being renovated? But I can't stand noisy builders hammering away all the time."

While Jasper and I waited for Mr. Lavington to finish at the front desk, I noticed the woman Mrs. Lavington had called Etta stood half-hidden behind another decorative vase filled with flowers. She gripped a small case that now I could see was a jewel case, which meant she was probably Mrs. Lavington's lady's maid. Her attention never wavered from the front doors, where the doorman stood looking out the window, watching for new arrivals, hands clasped behind his back.

Jasper said, "Your turn, Olive," drawing my attention. Ladies didn't normally sign hotel registers, but I stepped forward like the modern girl I was. I claimed my room key and signed with a flourish. The clerk told me my luggage would be delivered to my room and gave me the hours of the restaurant, then said, "The lift is in the hallway beside the stairs. Our lounge is located here on the ground floor through the doors opposite the restaurant. You can access the sun terrace from the first floor. Exit the lift, turn left, and go through the exterior door to the bridge."

I thanked him for the details and rejoined Jasper. He and Miss Ravenna were discussing snowshoe trails.

Jasper looked at me. "Shall we give snowshoeing a try while we're here? What do you say, old bean? Do you have a hankering to tramp through the woods in oversized footwear?"

"Why not? I'm sure the views would be lovely."

"Then let me give you a map of the trails." Miss Ravenna handed over a folded map with the creases worn to a softness that comes with use. "I found it quite handy last time we were here. Evert and I plan to ice-skate today. Shall we meet for dinner this evening?"

We agreed to gather in the lobby, and Miss Ravenna and Mr. Evert went to speak to the concierge about hiring ice skates. As Jasper tucked the map into his pocket, the doorman swung the front door wide, and the woman from the train with the dark curls, named Hattie, and her husband came in, followed by a bellboy with their bags. Hattie went straight to Mrs. Lavington. "Emmaline! You're staying here too? How wonderful! We can be together absolutely *all* the time."

The last thing I saw before I stepped into the small lift with Jasper was that Mrs. Lavington's social smile had a definite sour tinge.

Jasper pulled the grille across and punched the buttons on the panel. "I'll ride up to four with you first." He was on the third floor, and I was on the fourth. Once we were in motion, he said, "No snowshoeing for me today, I'm afraid. I'll be busy." He patted his suit jacket where he'd put away the map.

Miss Ravenna must have put something inside the folded map—whatever it was that Jasper was here to work on. "Don't worry about me. I assumed you'd be holed up in your room quite a bit."

"Only until I decipher the . . . map. Hopefully, it won't take me the whole holiday."

The lift stopped with a lazy bob at the fourth floor. The grille squeaked as Jasper pushed it open for me. I stepped out as I said, "I intend to stroll around and see the sights. I'll meet you back here for dinner." And I had a small task to complete.

CHAPTER 8

*A*fter changing into a jumper and a warm velvet circle skirt, I put on my knit cap and picked up my gloves and skates. Then I took a quick look around the hotel, stopping on the first floor to walk across the short bridge that connected the hotel to the sun terrace, which was enclosed with wood railings fashioned with the same decorative cut-out patterns as the hotel balconies. Chaise lounges lined the decking, all of them turned away from the hotel toward the mountain view.

The deep eaves of the hotel shaded the section of the terrace closest to the rear wall of the hotel, the overhang providing some shade for those who found the brilliant sun too intense. I added spending some time on the sun terrace to my mental list of things to do. I popped into the lounge, which had a small bar and scattered tables. No barman was on duty, and the room was quiet except for a woman knitting and a man snoring beside a dying fire at the far end of the room. My reconnaissance complete, I asked for directions to the police station and set out.

It was a short walk, and I mentally rehearsed what I would say. While I was not fluent in German—I had a better grasp of French—I could make myself understood. When I entered the police station and spoke to the officer on duty, I kept my sentences short and simple. I gave my name and said I had information I needed to share. The young man, whom I supposed would be the equivalent of an English constable, said, "Perhaps we switch to English, yes?"

"That would be nice. Thank you." I told him why I'd come and what I'd overheard. His eyebrows shot up when I mentioned the words *body* and *frozen ground*. He held up a finger. "Let me make a note." He took down my name and address in London, then had me repeat everything, which I did, but much slower as he transcribed it into his tiny printing. I also handed over the list of names that Jasper had procured from the train attendant.

The young man said, "Wait here a moment, please." I occupied myself, studying a map posted on the wall and ignored the gaze of another officer, an older man with a beefy build who seemed to find me more interesting than whatever he was typing. I glanced his way, and his attention returned to his work, the cadence of the typewriter becoming staccato.

The young man returned and asked me to follow him. He led me down a short hallway to an office, which was filled with the gentle strains of one of Chopin's sonatas. A man who looked to be in his late thirties or early forties came around his desk.

"Miss Belgrave, thank you for stopping in today. I am Korporale Vogel." He was small in stature, with a neat little mustache, a triangular beard, and faint wings of gray in the brown hair at his temples.

I was taken aback at the warmth in his tone, but I recovered and returned his greeting. I'd expected a stand-offish or suspicious reaction from the police, not this genial reception. It almost felt as if I were a friend who'd dropped by his house for a chat and some tea. Not that I was complaining. It certainly made a change from some of the more confrontational encounters I'd had with the police.

He turned down the music that flowed from a small radio on a credenza and gestured to a chair across from his desk. "Thank you, Oberwaller," he said to the young man in German, then switched to excellent English as he said to me, "Please have a seat, Miss Belgrave." He gave my name a faint questioning inflection.

"Yes, that's right. Olive Belgrave." He nodded, but he frowned briefly as he studied me. I thought he was about to say something else, but then he seemed to decide against it. His expression shifted to polite helpfulness. "How may I help you today?"

I really should have brushed up on my German before I departed, but then again, I hadn't expected I'd have a chat with the equivalent of a police officer—perhaps a police inspector?—on my first day in Switzerland. Once we were settled, Vogel placed his hand on the paper the younger officer had delivered to him as if he were about to swear on a Bible. "We appreciate you bringing this to our attention, Miss Belgrave. However, it's rather vague."

"I know, and I'm sorry that I can't provide more details."

"Yet you took the time during your first day in St. Moritz to visit the police."

"My conscience wouldn't let me rest easy until I'd passed it on to you."

"You are a good citizen." He could have infused the word with sarcasm—I knew some officers of the law who would have done that—but his tone was matter-of-fact. He leaned back in his chair and clasped his hands across his stomach. "I agree that what you heard is very ominous. You're sure there was nothing distinguishing about the voices? Or anything else that might identify the persons involved? Perhaps a scent? Perfume? Hair oil?"

I shook my head.

He persisted. "An accent?"

"No. And I've gone over it again and again in my mind. There was nothing like that. I'm sorry I can't be more definite or helpful."

He picked up the paper and ran his finger down the list of people who'd been in the carriage. "You're very thorough." His manner hadn't changed. It was still cordial, but he studied me with an assessing gaze.

I inched forward on my chair. Time for a little explanation. While reviewing my German, I'd also wrestled with how much to share with the police about myself. Complete disclosure seemed the best path. "I'll be straightforward with you, Korporale Vogel. I make my living by helping people who have problems—problems that they don't want to take to the police. I do this in England, of course. I've been involved in a few . . . incidents. Cases that involved crimes—some of them murder."

His eyebrows shot up. "Indeed?"

"Yes." I strove to keep any hint of apology out of my voice. I was proud of my contributions to solving those crimes, no matter how unorthodox my involvement had been. "I'm aware that having all the details can be important. I'm sure you'll want to look into my background. If you contact Inspector Longly at Scotland Yard, he can vouch for me."

I *hoped* he'd vouch for me. After all, my cousin Gwen was engaged to Inspector Longly. Being a future in-law surely had some benefits.

Vogel didn't write down the name. "And you are here on holiday, then? You're not"—he circled his fingers through the air, and finally came up with a word—"working?"

"Oh goodness, no. I'm here to enjoy the Alps. Ice-skate and perhaps try a bit of snowshoeing and possibly skiing, something I've never done."

"Then rest assured you can leave this with me." He tapped the list. "Don't think of it again. Enjoy your holiday here in our beautiful mountains."

He walked with me to the door, recommending the best snowshoeing trails, then said, "Good day, Miss Belgrave. Enjoy your visit."

I walked slowly up the hilly street, stepping carefully along the snow-packed path beside the road that I supposed in the summer was the pavement but was now invisible under a thick crystalline layer. I'd never had such a pleasant experience with the police. Had Vogel's politeness been a show? Now that I was gone, was he having a hearty laugh at me? Well, no matter. I'd felt compelled to turn over the information to them, and I had.

I passed houses and shops with wide eaves lined with

thick icicles that sometimes dripped on the back of my neck. I adjusted my coat collar and made a mental note to wear my scarf the next time I went out. Some of the buildings had murals painted on their stucco walls, everything from flags to folklore figures to geometric designs. As I labored up the slope of the street, a band seemed to squeeze my chest. I slowed my pace and pushed away the edge of panic that rose with the breathless feeling.

I wasn't used to the altitude, that was all. It would take a few days to become acclimated to it. I would need to take it easy in my skating. I popped into a few shops, which took my mind off my wheezy breathing. I rambled along, looking at tiny spoons and postcards until my breathing was normal. One must go home with a few bits and bobs after a trip abroad, but I'd return to the shops later to buy souvenirs.

At the rink, the ice glittered in the brilliant sunlight. I decided to make a few circuits to help me get acclimated, then I'd return to the hotel. I switched to my skates and took a few easy turns around the section cleared of snow, the blades of my skates rasping dully against the ice. With the snowy mountains as a background, it was easily the most beautiful place I'd ever skated—quite different from the small frozen ponds my cousins and I had swished across when we were growing up.

I caught snatches of laughter and chatter from other skaters as I whizzed by them, picking up speed. The wind sliced across my cheeks in a cold draft. I cut to the side to avoid a woman landing a toe loop with flair and clipped a man on the shoulder who was standing completely still.

"I'm so sorry. I—" I said as I circled back. "Oh, hello. I believe we were on the same train." It was the couple who'd come into breakfast that morning, the man with thinning ginger hair and a ruddy complexion and his wife, the petite black-haired woman called Hattie who Mrs. Lavington hadn't been thrilled to see.

As soon as I spoke to them, I realized I'd stumbled into an argument. They faced each other, faces set, shoulders tense. The atmosphere around them fairly crackled with suppressed anger.

I dug my toe into the ice, ready to murmur an apology as I glided backward, but another figure swooped up to our group and stopped with a graceful and compact half turn that kicked up a tiny spray of ice particles. Juliet had changed into a double-breasted velvet skating costume with a calf-length skirt. A Cossack-type fur hat rested on her auburn hair.

"Olive! It's wonderful to see you again," she said in a normal tone, as if the atmosphere on this little patch of the ice wasn't thick with angry words that had just been said. "And you've met Hattie and Rob Grogan? No? Oh, let me introduce you. We're all staying at the Alpine House, so we'll be seeing a lot of each other."

She performed the introductions, and the couple put smiles on their faces as we exchanged greetings. Juliet continued with her easy chatter. "Now that we all know each other, let's use first names, shall we? It makes it so much easier since we're staying at the same hotel. Of course, I'm not actually staying at the Alpine House proper. I'm in one of the hotel's chalets. It's up the mountain behind the hotel. I'm staying with Mrs. Ashford. Have you met her?"

"No, I haven't, but I'd like to make her acquaintance," I said. Hattie and Rob shook their heads. It seemed they couldn't wait for our little encounter to be over so they could resume their argument.

"I'll introduce you, Olive," Juliet said. "Drop by the lounge this evening. There's always a roaring fire going in there in the evening. Mrs. Ashford likes to *roast* there, as she calls it, while we go over paperwork. Can't say I blame her after all her time on the mountain crags. Oh, there's someone else you absolutely must meet." Juliet hooked her arm through mine, and I said goodbye to the Grogans as she towed me backward.

Once we were a few feet away, she said, "You looked like you were in need of a rescue."

"I was. Thank you. Ghastly to blunder into them and intrude like that. I'd obviously interrupted a quarrel."

"Probably about the shop."

"The shop?"

"The hat shop, LaRue's. Hattie owns it."

"Really? She's quite young to own a shop, isn't she? I've heard they have absolutely divine creations."

"I can confirm that is definitely the case." Juliet patted her fur hat. "I picked this up at LaRue's when I was in London last time. Quite dashing, isn't it, if I do say so myself."

I agreed. We were skating together, our long strokes matching as we breezed along. Juliet added, "I should have said Hattie *runs* LaRue's, but Emmaline put up the money to get it started. Whatever was Hattie thinking? Emmaline is such a mercurial creature. I can't imagine the strain of running a business with her looking over my shoulder all the time. A little birdie told me Hattie wants to buy out Emmaline, but Emmaline refuses to sell." She put a finger to her lips in a *shush* motion. "That's for your ears only. Don't go broadcasting it around."

"I'll keep it to myself," I said, my gaze going to the couple, who were now sitting on a bench, removing their skates. From their posture—stiffly angled away from each other—and their mulish expressions, it looked as if the argument wasn't over.

Juliet noticed the direction of my gaze. "Hattie and Rob are always having a spat, but they get through it. They have a feisty relationship."

"It seems rather serious."

"Don't worry about them. One can't be happy all the time."

CHAPTER 9

"Oh, it's snowing! How lovely," Miss Ravenna said later that evening as we emerged from the restaurant into the crisp mountain air that was as intoxicating as any cocktail. Tiny flakes were falling fast and thick.

"Isn't it?" I said. A new layer of pristine whiteness was already piling up on the trees, buildings, and motors. Jasper and I, along with Miss Ravenna and Mr. Vandenberg, had dined at another hotel that had music and dancing. Jasper was a divine partner, and if it hadn't been our first day at altitude we might have stayed longer.

Woodsmoke mingled with the scent of pine, and I drew in a deep breath of the biting air, glad to be out of the stuffy, smoky room. A layer of clouds hid the sky, and a light wind drove the snowflakes toward the buildings on the right-hand side of the street. The snow was already piling up on the pavement against the front of the hotel.

"You've had a long day," I said to the doorman as he swung the door wide for us to enter the Alpine House.

He touched the brim of his top hat, which sat right above his heavy brows. "All part of a day's work."

"Oh, you're British," I said, surprised by his accent.

His manner became less rote, and the expression on his square face became more animated. "Yes, miss. I grew up near Manchester."

"And do you find you like it here better than England, Mr. . . . "

"I'm Fredrick Klein, miss. One goes where one can find work."

"Indeed. Well, good evening."

"Shall we go through to the lounge?" Jasper asked once we were in the hotel lobby.

"Yes, let's." I unwound my scarf and removed my gloves. "Juliet said she'd introduce me to Mrs. Ashford this evening."

"A nightcap sounds lovely." Miss Ravenna shook the snow from her coat and handed it to a bellboy that the doorman had summoned. He took the rest of our coats and informed us they'd be sent up to our rooms. Mr. Vandenberg agreed to the suggestion of a nightcap, which didn't surprise me in the least.

I'd heard the phrase "dancing attendance on someone," but until this evening I'd never seen an example of it in real life. Vandenberg had ensured that Miss Ravenna wasn't too hot or too cold and that she was pleased with her seat at dinner. She only had to reach for her cigarette case, and Mr. Vandenberg had his lighter at the ready. After dinner, he'd swept Miss Ravenna around the dance floor until she said she was tired. Then I'd barely pushed back my chair and he was collecting our coats. His manner throughout the evening toward me had been polite but distant. At first, I'd thought he was shy, but as the night went on I changed my assessment of him. He was self-possessed and seemed completely comfortable to sit back and let Miss Ravenna, Jasper, and I dominate the conversation, only contributing occasionally.

Mr. Vandenberg pushed open the ornate wooden door to the hotel lounge for us. It was a long room with several tables near the bar at one end and a fire at the other with sofas and chairs grouped around it. Mrs. Ashford's evening gown had a fashionable, narrow silhouette, but the paisley cashmere shawl she drew around her shoulders was definitely Victorian. She gathered her handbag and shawl and stood. Juliet rose as well, brushing down the skirt of her evening gown.

Juliet's velvet dress was a deep magenta color with a dropped waist, fitted silk bodice, and tight, long sleeves of the velvety material. An overdress in a gauzy layer of tulle in the same color softened the rather severe lines of the gown. I had to admire the cleverness of the design. The velvet fabric and the long sleeves would keep Juliet warm, but the layer of tulle softened the look. A clip with a single feather in the same color held back her auburn hair on one side.

Hattie and Rob must have patched things up. They were at the other end of the lounge near the small semicircular bar, playing cards with Mr. and Mrs. Lavington. The atmosphere around the group seemed convivial. A low murmur of chatter punctuated by an occasional laugh came from the group. Juliet said something to Mrs. Ashford, then waved to us.

As we passed them, Mrs. Lavington, hand covering a yawn, looked up at a clock hanging on the wall, and her gaze caught mine. I nodded and smiled politely. We'd probably see quite a bit of each other during the next few days. Observing the social niceties would prevent any awkwardness. Mrs. Lavington gave me a minuscule nod.

Miss Ravenna and I led the way down the aisle that ran from the card table to the grouping of sofas and chairs by the fire. Juliet introduced me to Mrs. Ashford, and then I introduced everyone in our group to the two ladies. Once the formalities were out of the way, I pushed down a flutter of nerves and said, "Mrs. Ashford, I must tell you it's a thrill to meet you. I so admire what you've done. I read an article about you years ago, and it opened my eyes to the possibilities for women." I wasn't normally a gushy person, but I couldn't help myself.

"Excellent. Glad to hear it." The skin around Mrs. Ashford's deep-set eyes creased as she gave me a toothy grin. "And are you here to participate in winter sport, Miss Belgrave? Perhaps you ice-climb?"

"Oh no. I do skate, though. Perhaps I'll try snow-shoeing as well."

Juliet said, "Olive has had a few articles in the paper herself, Amy. She's a lady detective." I must have looked surprised because Juliet added, "I knew your name sounded familiar, but it took me a while to place you."

"Ah, now that is interesting." Mrs. Ashford tilted her head and studied me with more interest. "Perhaps you'd join me for tea one day? I must convince you to try ice-climbing."

"Tea sounds lovely. I'm not so sure about the ice-climbing."

Juliet said, "Amy's mission in life is to convert as many people as possible to mountaineering."

Mrs. Ashford raised her hand. "Not convert, Juliet, dear. Just give it a go. That's all I ask. The mountains do the work for me once I get people up there. There's no experience like it." Mrs. Ashford asked what our plans were for our time in St. Moritz and complimented Miss Ravenna on a recent film, then she said, "It would be delightful to stay and chat, but I must turn in as I have an early morning tomorrow."

"But only if the weather is clear?" Juliet asked. "It's begun to snow."

"Of course, my dear. I only go up when the guide agrees that it's safe. Pleasure to meet you all. Good night."

I invited Juliet to join our group, and we settled on the couches near the fire, which was roaring away, sending out an occasional pop. Mr. Vandenberg went off to get drinks for us.

Miss Ravenna turned to Jasper. "And how was your day? You've heard all about ours."

"It was good, although I'm sorry I missed out on joining you on the ice." Miss Ravenna and Mr. Vandenberg had spent the day skating, and her nose was pink from so much sun. Jasper continued, "Pity I have some work that must be dealt with. And still a ways to go." He looked to me. "No snowshoeing for me tomorrow, old bean, but don't let me hold you back."

"I'll see what the weather does." Thinking that Jasper and Miss Ravenna might need a moment to discuss what I'd begun to think of as their joint project, I shifted toward Juliet. "Do you snowshoe?"

"Yes, it's great fun, but I prefer skiing. Mrs. Ashford

prefers climbing, but there's nothing like the feeling of flying down the mountain on skis. You must try it while you're here."

"I'm afraid I might be *falling* down the mountain," I said and managed to fight off a yawn of my own. I angled my watch toward the fire so I could see the time. It showed ten minutes until ten. I'd stay a few more minutes —ten o'clock wasn't an impolite time to break up the group.

"You'd start small, of course," Juliet said, "on one of the gradual inclines—"

Across the room, a disgruntled exclamation came from Mrs. Lavington. She slung down her cards. "I do *hate* this horrid game."

Her voice carried, and everyone, including our group around the fire, looked her way.

"I'm sorry." She rubbed her temple and said in a more subdued tone, "I can't think. My head aches, and I'm exhausted." Her gaze went to the clock again. "I know it's early, but I'm retiring."

She stood and wrapped a fur stole around her shoulders. Mr. Lavington crushed his cigarette into the ashtray as he pushed back his chair, but she put a hand on his shoulder. "No, don't come with me. I won't spoil your evening. I know you'd like to play another round." She put the back of her hand over her mouth as another yawn came over her. She shook her head, a sharp motion, as if she were fighting off the Sandman. "I just need silence and quiet." She left the lounge, the skirt of her gold lamé gown whispering across the carpet.

Hattie looked our way and raised her voice. "Anyone fancy joining us for bridge?"

Juliet turned to me, her expression eager. "Go ahead," I said. "I'm so tired I'm sure I'd muddle something. I intend to go upstairs in a moment."

"I may muddle something myself, but I never turn down a challenge." She sprang up. "Would anyone else want to join in? We'd almost have enough for another table. I'm sure I can find a fourth for a second group."

"No, you go ahead," I said. Miss Ravenna and Jasper were in deep conversation, and I knew Mr. Vandenberg would go along with whatever Miss Ravenna wanted.

"All right, if you're sure." The lightweight tulle fabric billowed around the long sleeves and fluttered around her skirt as she crossed the room. Mr. Vandenberg, hands full with the drinks for us all, nodded at Juliet as they passed each other in the aisle. Juliet took the seat Mrs. Lavington had vacated. "I hope I don't let you down, Mr. Lavington."

"Oh, I don't think you will." He offered his cigarette case around the group. Hattie and Juliet both took one as Mr. Lavington added, "We should give these two a run for their money."

I took my drink from Mr. Vandenberg and turned my attention away from the bridge players. Jasper and Miss Ravenna had completed their rather cryptic conversation, and our discussion shifted to travel—hotel recommendations and details about train schedules.

I was seated closest to the dancing flames of the fire. The heat coming off the fire was intense, wrapping me in a cocoon of warmth. The shuffle of cards, an occasional groan of disbelief, and a celebratory laugh were the only sounds coming from the bridge players. My eyelids dipped to half-mast, but the fire popped, and I startled.

I'd asked Mr. Vandenberg to bring me a mineral water,

and I picked it up from the little table and took a great gulp. I sat up straighter and glanced around to see if anyone else had noticed I'd almost fallen asleep, which was terribly bad manners. Fortunately, no one had noticed my faux pas.

The muted click of cards being played continued from the far end of the room. Jasper and Mr. Vandenberg had discovered they had both visited Innsbruck at the same time, and they were trying to sort out if they could have possibly met at a certain event there. Miss Ravenna was focused on Mr. Vandenberg, watching him in a way that made me think her publicity team would have a difficult time if they were to continue to portray her as a cool, aloof blonde.

The cards riffled as Mr. Lavington shuffled. Juliet lit another cigarette, and I was glad I was across the room from the group. Hattie and Rob pushed back their chairs. Hattie picked up her handbag and left, and Rob followed her out. A little while later, Hattie returned alone. She must have gone to the powder room because a fresh coat of red brightened her lips. A moment later Rob crossed the threshold, bearing two gin and tonics. "Sorry. Had to go to the bar in the restaurant because the one in here closes early."

I was just about to make my excuses and go upstairs to bed when Miss Ravenna said to me, "Evert and I are planning to snowshoe tomorrow. I heard the trail that goes around the lake is beautiful. You're welcome to join us."

I didn't want to be a gooseberry. "I'm not sure yet what my plans are for tomorrow."

"Oh, do come. If you'd rather not snowshoe, we could take a sleigh ride—"

A shriek came from the card table. I knew immediately it wasn't something to do with the game. There was something visceral and raw about the noise that jerked everyone's attention to the bridge table.

CHAPTER 10

*J*uliet pushed back from the table and let out another panicked cry. A flame flickered across the fine gauzy fabric that covered the fitted sleeve of her gown.

Hattie screamed and flinched backward. Mr. Lavington and Rob jumped up and tried to get to Juliet, but they collided with each other as Juliet flailed her arm and lurched away from the table. Her jerky movements increased the flames as she stumbled down the aisle toward us.

Mr. Vandenberg, who was seated across from me, was closest to Juliet and sprang up. He lunged by me, snatched up the hearthrug, and wrapped it around Juliet. She struggled, thrashing about, and they fell to the floor as Mr. Vandenberg tried to keep the rug around her. Mr. Lavington shouted something about getting help and sprinted from the room.

I jumped up and dashed to the bar. I jerked cupboard doors open until I found a pitcher, then I filled it with water at a small sink. But by the time I rushed back, the flames were out. Juliet, still bundled in the rug, lay breathing hard, her eyes glassy with tears. Her face was the ashy color of the snow at the edges of the streets. She whispered, "It's out. Thank goodness. It's out."

Jasper had snatched up a cushion and was beating at the smoldering fire on the fabric of a chair that Juliet had bumped. I dumped the water onto the chair. I waved away the plumes of acrid smoke that hung in the air.

His energetic movements had caused Jasper's hair to fall forward. He tossed the cushion aside and swiped his hair off his forehead. "You're a brick, Olive. Well done."

"You're welcome, old bean," I said, my voice shaky. "Grigsby would be in tizzy if he could see you." Smudges of ash marred Jasper's crinkled white shirtfront.

He tugged his sleeves back into alignment. "Thankfully, he's not here to see the damage."

Mr. Vandenberg had sat back on his heels, and he looked almost as gray and shaken as Juliet. Miss Ravenna stepped over and knelt on the other side of Juliet, who was now struggling to push the rug away and sit up.

Miss Ravenna put a hand on her shoulder, which peeked out above the wrapping of the rug. "Stay for a moment. You've had a shock." I returned to the bar, passing by Rob and Hattie, who huddled together. Rob, arm around Hattie, was rubbing her shoulder. She sounded as if she was in shock too because she was murmuring in a low, singsong voice, "It was her cigarette. I saw her sleeve touch it as she reached for the scoresheet. I tried to say something, but the fire just bloomed and raced along the fabric."

Rob's voice was low and soothing. "There's nothing

you could have done. Juliet's fine. The fire's out. Everything is fine now."

I put down the pitcher and filled a glass from the tap. A spray of frigid water hit my hand. I flinched and wiped the back of my hand on my skirt as I went back to the other end of the room and kneeled beside Miss Ravenna.

Juliet had ignored Miss Ravenna and was now sitting, her back propped against one end of a sofa. She'd pushed the rug away and was examining her sleeves. "How are you?" I asked as I held out the glass.

She took it with her left hand while she twisted her right arm this way and that. "Amazingly, I'm all right. Wobbly, but other than that, I'm fine."

"Completely understandable." Miss Ravenna took Juliet's hand and examined her from the tips of her fingers up to her shoulder. A few bits of the charred tulle fabric remained, and the velvet was singed at the cuff, but Mr. Vandenberg's quick thinking had prevented the flames from burning completely through the fabric of her sleeve. "You're a very lucky young lady," Miss Ravenna pronounced.

Juliet looked up at Mr. Vandenberg, who was hovering. "Thanks to Mr. Vandenberg. I saw those flames and went batty."

"I think we all did." His diction wasn't as perfect as it had been, and his accent came through a little bit stronger.

"But you saved me," Juliet said. "I don't know how to thank you."

He lifted a hand, fingers splayed, and waved off her statement. "I just happened to be near to the rug."

"And had the presence of mind to grab it and suffocate

the flames," Miss Ravenna added. If she hadn't been in love with Mr. Vandenberg before, I think his actions combined with his self-deprecating attitude would have tipped her over the edge. Of course, she'd been looking at him in an adoring way all night, but now that look intensified.

Jasper had moved to the windows and was throwing back the drapes and opening the casements. It was only then that I realized my eyes were stinging and my throat felt tight.

Juliet sipped the water, then handed the glass back to me, and I asked, "Would you like more water or something stronger?"

"No, thank you." She shifted to stand up, and Mr. Vandenberg and Miss Ravenna each took one of her arms to steady her.

A commotion, a babble of raised voices sounded outside the door, and then a man with a flushed face and bleary eyes lurched into the room and shouted in a Yorkshire accent, "Fire! Everyone out!"

"You're a bit late to the party, old thing." Jasper went across to him. "Calm yourself, man. Fire's out. There's no need to cause a stampede."

"But—there's smoke and you know that old saying—" The cadence of loud footfalls and more shouts carried from beyond the door.

Jasper turned the man by his shoulder and set him in motion out the door. "Yes, but in this case the fire is out, as I said." Jasper, hand on the man's shoulder, maneuvered him into the lobby. Jasper's raised voice carried over the commotion. "Everything's fine. There's no fire. No need to leave the hotel."

Jasper returned with a short, stocky man with spectacles. Jasper introduced him as Mr. Hoffman, the hotel proprietor. I'd seen Mr. Hoffman several times throughout the day, and each time he'd had a pleasant and welcoming smile on his face, but now his brows were smashed together in an anxious frown. He went straight to Juliet and said in his German-accented English, "We will call for a doctor immediately. Please be seated. Or perhaps you'd rather go to your room?"

She shook her head. "There's no need for that, I assure you." He was about to argue, but Juliet continued, "Honestly, there's no need for a fuss—or any more of a fuss than I've already caused. I was so frightened. I screamed and caused quite a scene." She showed him her arm. "I'm perfectly fine. There's no need to call for a doctor. I'm very sorry for causing so much trouble, and of course I'll pay for the damage." She motioned to the soaked chair and the wrinkled and charred rug.

"Out of the question," Mr. Hoffman said firmly. "Please go and rest, and this will be taken care of."

"No, I insist," Juliet said. "It was my own carelessness that caused this. I should have kept my sleeve away from the cigarette."

"And I insist most strongly that we will take care of everything," Mr. Hoffman countered.

Juliet agreed, then she turned to Hattie and Rob and included our group in her glance as well. "I'm done in. I believe I'll retire upstairs."

Miss Ravenna looped her arm through Juliet's. "I'll go up and stay with you until a maid arrives to help you change."

"That's very kind of you."

Mr. Vandenberg went to call the lift for the two women. While Juliet had rallied and her complexion had returned to a healthy tone, Hattie still seemed to be stunned. She leaned into her husband's side as they left the lounge. Jasper looked at me with raised eyebrows. "Ready to call it a night?"

With the windows open, the temperature in the room had plummeted. Although the snow had stopped falling, the freezing alpine air had filtered into the room. I'd been inching closer to the fire to stay warm, although I couldn't look at it without thinking of the flames racing along Juliet's sleeve, which gave me a sick feeling in the pit of my stomach. "Oh yes." I said, taking his arm.

We were crossing the lobby when Mr. Lavington burst in through the main doors, bringing with him the smell of snow and a blast of biting air. He hurried over. "I couldn't find the doctor." His words were breathy.

"Everything's fine," Jasper said. "It was only her sleeve. She wasn't burned at all."

Mr. Lavington leaned over and braced his hands on his knees while he caught his breath. After a moment, he straightened. "The doorman told me where the doctor lived. I thought it would be best to go directly there and get help. I thought she would need . . . someone right away."

His voice caught on the last phrase. He swallowed. "Sorry. I'm shaken up. I've never seen anything as horrible as that."

"It was grim." Jasper clapped Mr. Lavington on the shoulder. "Let's get you a drink, warm you up. I think a brandy is in order."

Mr. Lavington hesitated, then said, "Well, all right. A quick one."

Jasper looked at me inquiringly, but I shook my head. "I'll see you tomorrow at breakfast."

The two men headed for the bar, while I went upstairs. After the draftiness of the lounge, it was delightful to step inside my cozy room. The Swiss did know how to do heating properly.

The burst of energy I'd felt earlier as I sprinted back and forth with the water pitcher had drained away. A weariness settled over me like a heavy cloak weighing on my shoulders. I would have liked to snuggle under the coverlet and layers of blankets, but I hadn't unpacked.

My suitcase rested on my bed, clothes muddled from where I'd hurriedly pulled out changes of clothes for skating and later for dinner. If I had a maid, she would have already tidied everything away, but since I was a modern young woman—dashing and adventurous—who traveled sans maid, there was no one to clear away the mess except me. There were definitely times when being a modern working girl had its downsides.

I picked up a skirt, shook it out, and hung it in the large wardrobe. I worked my way through the clothes, folding jumpers, hanging up blouses, and soothing the wrinkles from my other fancy evening frock. I tucked away my shoes, boots, and skates, aligning them across the bottom of the wardrobe, then I picked up my sponge bag and dressing gown and opened my door to go down the hall to the bath.

Mr. Lavington was trotting up the stairs, and I nodded to him as I stepped out of my room. He hurried over. "Miss Belgrave, a moment, please." He surged up on his tiptoes, looking over my shoulder into my room. "Is Emmaline with you?"

The brandy on his breath wafted my way. "No. I haven't seen her since she left the lounge."

He dropped back down to his normal height and rubbed his forehead, which furrowed with a frown. With a faint trace of stubble shadowing his face and rumpled evening kit, which had a torn seam at the shoulder, he didn't look as clean-cut and sharply dressed as he had this morning on the train. "I haven't either. I don't know where Emmaline could be. She's not in our room. She's not with Hattie. She's not in the lobby or lounge or restaurant. I thought perhaps she might have come along to your room."

I pushed the door wide. "I'm sorry, but she's definitely not here."

"Oh." His shoulders rounded. "She told me she'd met you on the train. I thought perhaps . . ." He stepped back from my door, his hands dropping limply to his sides. "I don't know where else she could be." He looked bone-weary. He had been running around, searching for a doctor, but there was something more than exhaustion in his movements. His concerned look had deepened into worry.

I wondered if Mrs. Lavington hadn't actually been feeling ill. She might have had a meeting with her blackmailer. I didn't voice my thoughts aloud. She'd asked for me to keep mum, and even though she wasn't a client, I wouldn't betray her confidence. "You might ask the concierge or Mr. Hoffman if they've seen her. Perhaps she stepped out for a breath of fresh air. Or maybe she's out for a stroll."

A small smile cracked through his worried demeanor. "Emmaline doesn't stroll—or do *any* sort of exercise actually. And she especially wouldn't go for stroll on a snowy night." He straightened. "But seeing as there's nothing else to do, I'll check with them. Thank you, Miss Belgrave. Sorry to have disturbed you."

I closed the door to my room and walked to the bath. I went through my nightly ablutions, then returned to my room. Flushed and pink from a quick soak in a steamy bath, my room now felt stifling. I tugged open the drapes and cracked the French door to the balcony. I lingered a moment, breathing the champagne-like glacial air.

Somewhere below me, the words of a woman with an American accent drifted up from another balcony. " . . . either too hot or too cold . . . absurd they can't . . . regulate—"

I reached for the handle to close the door, but then the woman gasped as her words broke off. Her voice changed, ringing with an urgency that made me pause. "Betrand, come here."

The bass reply was short, and apparently negative, because the woman spoke again, her tone sharper and commanding. "No, you *must* come look." Her voice became louder as she continued, "There's a woman down on the terrace, and she's hurt. Come see, and then go down to the front desk and tell someone."

Inhaling wisps of cold air through the gap in the door was a completely different experience than stepping onto the balcony in only a dressing gown and slippers. Freezing air assaulted my bare ankles, hands, and face. Snow crunched under the thin soles of my slippers, and my feet went icy cold as I tiptoed to the railing and looked over.

The snow had stopped, and only a few wisps of clouds lingered. The light from the stars and a full moon, along with the brightening effect of the layer of snow, made it easy to see the terrace below. I stepped back from the snow-covered wooden handrail as a wave of light-headedness hit me. I recognized the golden lamé dress and the fur stole.

CHAPTER 11

*T*he voices of the man and the woman below me carried on, but they'd faded to an indistinguishable murmur. I inched forward again to make sure I hadn't imagined the horrible sight. I leaned against the balcony's handrail, oblivious to the bite of the snow that soaked into my dressing gown. Mrs. Lavington had been sitting in one of the chaise lounges, which were arranged in rows across the terrace with little tables spaced between each one. She must have been sitting in the lounger along the back of the terrace near the hotel. It looked as if she'd tumbled off the chair and landed on her side. Her handbag rested on the empty chaise.

The falling snow had created a thin layer over her, partially filling her trail of footprints across the terrace and blurring the bright gold of her dress, the dark fur of her stole, and the shine of her blonde hair. The cascade of falling flakes masked everything except the scarlet stain beside her head.

Something long and narrow sparkled near Mrs.

Lavington—an icicle, I realized. It was partially covered by snow, but I could still distinguish the long cylindrical shape that narrowed to a sharp point, which lay in the crimson pool. I shifted my gaze from that disturbing image. Several icicles were scattered along the edge of the terrace, sprinkled over the lounges in the back row.

I tilted my head up. A row of icicles, some six or seven inches long, hung from the eaves in a spiky fringe, except for a few sections which were completely clear. The empty spaces alternating with the icicles gave the impression of a gap-toothed snarl of a monster, like something out of Grimm's fairy tales.

I went back to my room, brushed a few sodden flakes away from the snow-soaked line on my dressing gown. I closed the French doors and stood there a moment, leaning against the cold panes of glass as I buried my freezing hands in the pockets of my gown.

I hadn't particularly liked Mrs. Lavington, but what a ghastly thing to happen. To be struck by an icicle, of all things! There was no doubt in my mind that she was dead. The stillness of her limbs and the amount of blood—I shut down that line of thought.

I took off my slippers, found a pair of wool socks, yanked them on, and then shoved my feet into my boots. I pulled my coat on over my dressing gown and snatched up my room key, hurrying down the stairs to the lobby, not wanting to wait on the lift.

I was descending from the second floor and had just rounded the landing when a door creaked below, and a blast of arctic air swirled up the staircase. I paused, hand on the railing, and looked over the railing to the first floor. Mr. Hoffman stepped inside, then held open the door that gave access to the little bridge that ran from the hotel to the terrace.

A portly, balding man in a dressing gown and slippers entered, and Mr. Hoffman came in behind him. I was far enough up the stairs that neither man noticed me. Mr. Hoffman locked the door as he said, "My sincere apologies. Thank you for making me aware of the situation." He pulled back the grate on the lift and gestured for the man to step inside. "Please return to your room. I'm sure there won't be any need for any—ah—officials—to speak to you. Everything will be handled discreetly. Again, I apologize for the disruption of your holiday. Good night." After the guest stepped in, Mr. Hoffman leaned in, punched the button for the man's floor, and closed the grate.

I continued down the stairs to the first floor and went to Mr. Hoffman. "I saw what happened," I gestured to the door to the terrace, "from my balcony."

"There's nothing to be done. I apologize that your evening has been disturbed, Miss Belgrave." He grimaced. "Again. Please return to your room. The doctor is on his way, and I've summoned Korporale Vogel."

"The police? Then you think there was . . ." I trailed off, not sure if he was familiar with the phrase *foul play*.

But he understood the question in my unfinished sentence and shook his head. "No, no. Nothing like that. It was an accident. She was alone on the terrace. There was only one set of footprints in the snow. It was a terrible, terrible accident."

I looked down at the parquet floor, reviewing the scene in my mind. Yes, he was right. A single trail of footprints had run from the little bridge, across the terrace, to the chaise lounge. I'd been so shocked at seeing Mrs.

Lavington lying there motionless with the pool of blood beside her that the solitary line of footprints hadn't registered.

Mr. Hoffman massaged the space between his eyebrows and spoke to himself more than to me as he continued, "Two tragedies in one evening. *Two!* First, the fire, and now this—a guest dead in a dreadful accident. All in one day. The hotel will never recover from this. Never."

"But it's not your fault if a guest is careless with a cigarette. And, as you just said, what happened to Mrs. Lavington was an accident."

A hint of doubt crept into my words as I spoke of Mrs. Lavington. He jerked his hand away from his face. "Oh, without a doubt." He gestured to the roof. "You can see the gap where the icicles fell, right above her chair. It's never happened *here*, of course, but it's not unheard of. A few years ago, a man walking through town was struck by a falling icicle. He's a relative of one of the bellboys. He had to have seven stitches in his neck. Another time, years and years ago, a woman staying in a nearby village died after an icicle struck her on the head—like the situation we have here with Mrs. Lavington."

"I had no idea that could happen."

"It's a rare thing."

"Mr. Lavington was looking for his wife earlier. Has he been informed about . . . ?" I angled my head toward the door to the terrace.

"No, and that must be done." Mr. Hoffman rubbed the bridge of his nose, then he scanned the lobby, which was empty except for hotel staff.

My thoughts clicked through the people we'd met, searching for someone who could be with Mr. Lavington, someone who could perhaps break the news to him, but none of my new acquaintances seemed to be especially close with the Lavingtons. Rob hadn't even spoken to Mr. Lavington on the train, and we'd seen the two young climbers, Blinkhorn and Hale, earlier in the evening at the restaurant. They had said they were on their way to another restaurant, the Koller. Jasper had said it was more like a pub and was a bit rowdy. I wondered if they were back. Even if they were, the atmosphere between Mr. Lavington and the young men was more the nature of a teacher with students. I wasn't sure they'd be much of a comfort to him. A contemporary would be better.

"Perhaps you might send for Mr. Rimington and ask him to break the news. He's good in a crisis. I'd summon him myself, but I only know he's on the third floor, not which room he's in."

Mr. Hoffman looked relieved at the suggestion. He called one of the hotel attendants and sent him on the errand, then his gaze focused on a point behind me. "Ah, Korporale Vogel."

Vogel trotted up the stairs and greeted Mr. Hoffman in German. "Miss Belgrave, isn't it?" Vogel asked, switching to his excellent English. His eyebrows wrinkled together in a quizzical look as he took in my boots peeping out from my dressing gown, which traced along the floor below the hem of my coat.

He must have been dining out because he was in evening kit. I wished I'd taken a few moments to change into proper clothing before I'd come down to the lobby. "Yes, that's right." I pulled the lapels of my coat closer. "Please forgive my rather odd attire. I saw what happened and came down to see if there was anything I could do."

"And what has happened?" Vogel looked to Mr. Hoffman.

"One of our guests has been struck by a falling icicle." He tugged a key from his waistcoat pocket and unlocked the door to the terrace. "This way."

"It's Mrs. Lavington," I added, and Vogel's steps checked. "And you have some . . . information, Miss Belgrave? Something you'd like to share about this?"

"About Mrs. Lavington in particular. It might relate to the situation on the terrace." I wasn't sure if it did, but I had to tell him about the blackmail. What had once been privileged information had to be shared with the police now.

He frowned. "I see. Please wait here in the lobby."

I was debating running up and changing out of my dressing gown when the lift glided down and bounced to a stop. Jasper pulled back the squeaky grate. He'd changed into trousers and a jumper. "Hello, old bean. Now that is an avant-garde look. Out to set a new style?"

"Nothing so dramatic as that."

"Couldn't sleep? I must say that I've never had a woman summon me to the lobby in the middle of the night."

I smiled at his teasing tone, then turned serious. "I'm afraid it's for a tragic reason."

I told him about Mrs. Lavington, and Jasper's expression sobered. "I say, what a beastly thing to happen."

"Yes, isn't it? The doctor has been called. The police are on the terrace now."

Jasper had been surveying the lobby, but his gaze zinged back to me. "The police?"

"Mr. Hoffman says injuries from falling icicles are

rare, but they do happen. Apparently, summoning the police is a standard thing to do when someone dies unexpectedly."

"Yes, that would be the case in England as well. But then, why are you here in the lobby?"

"Mrs. Lavington shared something with me that Korporale Vogel should know. I'm to wait here and speak to him later."

"I see. Something she said to you on the train, I imagine. But that's not something you'd need my help with."

"No, I'm quite capable of speaking to the korporale on my own. Someone will have to break the news to Mr. Lavington."

It took Jasper only a beat to catch on. "Oh, it's me, is it?"

"I thought it would be better than Mr. Hoffman or one of the climbers. Mr. Lavington doesn't seem to have any close friends here."

Jasper drew in a breath and gave a short little nod, accepting the commission. "I'll help in whatever way I can. Although there's not much one can do in a situation like this."

"Perhaps just sit with him until the police are ready to speak to him?"

"Yes, of course. Where is Mr. Hoffman? Has he summoned Mr. Lavington as well?"

"No, not yet. Here's Mr. Hoffman and the korporale."

The two men returned from the terrace. I introduced Jasper to Vogel, who greeted him cordially, but clearly he was preoccupied and quickly nodded his agreement to the suggestion that Jasper break the news to Mr. Lavington. Then Vogel turned to a police officer who'd just arrived, the young man who'd manned the front desk at the police station. His jacket was buttoned incorrectly and his eyelids were droopy.

"Ah, Oberwaller, there you are," Vogel said. "Get a cup of coffee, then stay here by the door. Only let the doctor through. Once Swartz arrives, let him take over here. Come down and find me. You speak English. I'll need you to take notes. Miss Belgrave, I'll speak to you soon."

Jasper and Mr. Hoffman went up in the lift to speak to Mr. Lavington, and I went to the lobby to find a chair. It was going to be a long night.

CHAPTER 12

A constant stream of officials, including a doctor, by the look of the small black bag the man carried, filled the lobby while I waited. The boost of energy that had sent me flying down the stairs seeped away, and I drifted off at some point. I woke with a crick in my neck from sleeping with my head against the wing of the chair.

Hoffman put his office at Vogel's disposal, and a short time later, while Mr. Lavington was ensconced there with the korporale, the body of Mrs. Lavington, now covered with a thick drape, was carried out through the lobby.

Jasper had come to sit beside me while waiting for Mr. Lavington, and we exchanged a silent glance at the sad sight. A moment later Mr. Lavington came out of the office. He stopped near the front desk and stood there swaying, his gaze unfocused. Oberwaller requested Jasper follow him. Korporale Vogel wanted to speak to him next. Mr. Lavington didn't look up or acknowledge Jasper as he passed by him.

I went over to him. "Mr. Lavington, why don't you have a seat over here by me?" He didn't respond, but when I took his arm and guided him to a chair, he shuffled along like an automaton. Once he was seated, I went back to the desk and said to the clerk, "Find Mr. Hoffman and tell him Mr. Lavington needs someone to help him to his room."

"Right away, miss." I had to give credit to Mr. Hoffman. His staff was so well trained that the man didn't even blink or look twice at my strange coat-over-a-dressing-gown ensemble.

I went back and sat down beside Mr. Lavington. He'd taken out a lighter and his cigarette case, his movements jerky. The case was empty. He stared at it a moment, then seemed to come out of his hazy state. "Might I borrow a cigarette from you, Miss Belgrave?"

"I don't smoke, but I'm sure the hotel—" I turned to look for another attendant, but Mr. Lavington cut me off.

"No, don't trouble yourself." He snapped the case closed and returned it and the lighter to his pocket with trembling fingers, then leaned forward, elbows on his knees, and rested his forehead on the heels of his hands.

I sat beside him for a few moments, wondering if he was silently crying, but his shoulders weren't shaking. After a bit, he sat up abruptly. "Why did she go out there? Out to the terrace?" Before I could reply, he went on. "Why didn't she go up to our room?" He sniffed, blinked rapidly, and let out a tiny laugh. "Of course, Emmaline never does—did—what was expected. Impetuous, that was Emmaline. She couldn't abide plans and schedules. Said they were too, too dreadfully dull." His words hitched on the last sentence. He cleared his throat, his Adam's apple working.

"I'm so sorry."

"Thank you." He dropped his head back into his hands and sat hunched over until Jasper emerged from the office. Mr. Hoffman arrived at the same time and suggested Mr. Lavington retire. Jasper murmured to Mr. Hoffman that he'd take care of Mr. Lavington, then he tapped him on the shoulder. "Come on, Lavington. I'll walk up with you."

A police officer, an older, burly man with a pencil mustache, who I supposed was probably the equivalent of a sergeant, asked me to come with him. He ushered me to a seat on the other side of the desk from Vogel, who was on a telephone call. The younger officer, Oberwaller, was in the corner of the room with a pencil and pad of paper at the ready. Vogel covered the receiver and said, "Thank you, Swartz. I'll need to speak to Mr. Hoffman next." The stocky older officer left, and Vogel went back to his telephone conversation.

". . . tomorrow, then," he said. "Discreetly. No need for the word to get out any sooner than it must." He ended the called and rubbed his eyes before turning to me. "Let's have your full name and address in England, Miss Belgrave." His diction was still excellent, but now the trace of his German accent was a shade stronger. The late hour was taking a toll on him as well.

I refrained from pointing out that I'd given him the information during my visit to the police station. I felt saggy, as if I were dragging around weights when I moved. The bags under Vogel's eyes indicated he felt the same way, and he hadn't had the benefit of a catnap. I gave the information, then said, "It's late, and I know you're busy, so I'll get straight to the point—"

"In a moment." Vogel smoothed his hand over his Van Dyke beard. "First, let's get down the particulars. Did you see Mrs. Lavington this evening before going up to your room?"

"Yes, in the lounge."

"What time?" His questions were rote, his tone mild, as if he wasn't really interested in my answers.

"I'm not sure. Between nine and a quarter to ten, I think. We'd been to dinner and danced." I listed the members of our group, then said, "I spoke to the doorman on the way inside. He might be able to give you an exact time."

The pencil scritched against the paper as Oberwaller took notes. Vogel waited, blinking his eyes in an exaggerated way, as if to ward off sleepiness. When the other man looked up, finished with his transcription, Vogel twitched his shoulders and shifted in the chair. "And did you speak to Mrs. Lavington tonight?"

"No, she was with the bridge players. Our group was at the other end of the room."

Vogel took up a pen and rolled it back and forth between the palms of his hands as he watched me. "I see. Did you overhear anything from her group?"

"Not much. Some comments about the cards. Although I did hear her say her head ached and she was going upstairs."

"What was her demeanor?"

"She seemed upset with the game—frustrated—and I heard her say she was tired. She yawned several times.

She left right after that. Oh, and I noticed she glanced at the clock a few times."

He yawned, and I found myself doing the same thing. Just speaking the word seemed to bring them on, especially at this hour of the night. "Pardon me," Vogel said. "What time was it that she left?"

"Ten till ten."

"You're sure about that?"

"Yes, I checked the time because I was considering if it would be impolite to go upstairs as well. I'm not acclimated to the altitude yet. I was done in."

"But you were on your balcony later? It's rather chilly to be outside." The question surprised me. It was at odds with his languid tone and lethargy.

I straightened. While his tone was causal, his questions were much more detailed than I'd expected. "My room was stuffy. I opened the door to the balcony to get some fresh air. I heard a woman on one of the floors below me complaining about the same thing, then she called to her husband and said someone was hurt on the terrace. That was shortly after I saw Mr. Lavington in the hallway. He was looking for his wife. He seemed worried." I recounted the short exchange. The officer taking notes finished writing down what I'd said and looked up, but Vogel sat, his gaze abstracted as he moved the pen back and forth, the metal of the pen clicking against the ring he wore.

Then the korporale yawned again, scrubbed his hand over his beard, and tossed the pen on the desk. "How long have you known Mrs. Lavington?"

"I met her on the train. That's what I wanted to speak to you about. We met in the dining car that morning. Mr. Rimington introduced us, and Mrs. Lavington asked to speak to me privately. When she came to my compartment, she told me she'd heard about my work. She wanted to hire me because she was being blackmailed."

Vogel stared at me for a long moment, then lowered his chin, nearly tucking it into his collar. "Indeed?"

"Yes. I don't know why she was being blackmailed, but she'd had several demands for money within the last year. She'd received one on the train." I summarized the details Mrs. Lavington had told me about the blackmail and how I'd declined to take her on as a client. Vogel watched me while the officer scribbled away. When the scratch of the pencil stopped, Vogel said, "I'm surprised you turned her down."

"As I said, I didn't think we'd work well together. She wanted things done a certain way."

"Her way?"

"Yes. We had a difference of opinion on how to handle the case. I told her it would be better for her to find someone who agreed with her idea of how it should be done."

Vogel's gaze went to the clock on the wall. The long hand was ticking toward a quarter to three. "And why are you telling me this?"

"Well, Mrs. Lavington died unexpectedly. I felt I had to share the information in the event that it relates somehow to her death."

He waved to Oberwaller behind me, dismissing him. Once the door closed behind him, Vogel began stacking papers. "I contacted Inspector Longly earlier today." He tapped the papers on the desk into alignment. "This is not a case for you. This is an accidental death."

"Death by icicle?"

"It's infrequent, I'll grant you that. It only happens in . . . what do you English say? A brown moon?"

"Once in a blue moon."

"Yes, that is it. Blue moon."

"But you have to find Mrs. Lavington's death *slightly* suspicious. The blackmail—"

"Which we only have your word for." His tone was conversational, not threatening, but his comment silenced me and shifted my perspective. My intention was to be helpful. To Vogel, I was an annoyance—a possibly suspicious annoyance at that. Young ladies of my class did not involve themselves in this type of situation.

He gestured to the map on the wall. It showed St. Moritz nestled in the valley encircled with towering peaks. "Visitors think only of winter sport when they come here, but the mountains are dangerous. Brutal, even. There is a primitive wildness here, an unpredictability that one simply cannot overcome. There was only one set of footprints on the sun terrace. If someone else had been on the terrace, an additional set of footprints would be visible. The snow stopped falling at a quarter to ten. I can vouch for that personally. I noticed because I left a dinner party at that time to make my way home."

"But someone could reach the terrace from the balconies above. The second floor is probably only six feet above the terrace."

"The snow on all the balcony railings was undisturbed. I checked." He gave me a smile of the type that long-suffering parents show to their children when their patience is tried. "As was the snow on the roof and on the ground all around the terrace." He pushed back his chair, a signal that the conversation—or whatever it was, interview or interrogation—was over.

I stood. "And what about the blackmailer?" I really should learn how to let things go, but I couldn't help pushing a bit more.

Vogel put his pen away in his tailcoat pocket. "*If* that person exists, then I'm sure when the news gets out, I imagine they will be quite sad because their target is no longer alive." Vogel came around the desk and held the door. "Thank you for your time. Good evening, Miss Belgrave."

CHAPTER 13

*T*he next morning I paused at the end of the hallway and pushed back the curtain of the window that looked out over the front of the hotel. As the sun pushed up over the mountains, golden light spilled into the basin of the valley, reflecting off the cleared icy sections of the lake like light flashing on a silver tray. I went downstairs and was surprised to find the door to the terrace unlocked.

I pushed through and walked across the bridge, arms crossed to keep warm. I hadn't brought a coat because I'd expected the terrace to be closed off. There was no sign that a woman had died there a few hours ago. Footprints crisscrossed the snow that covered the wood decking. The chairs and tables were stacked to the side, and the blood had been cleaned away.

Despite the sunshine, the terrace was deserted. It was too early for sun-worshipers. I walked to the area next to the railing that had been cleaned. A few feet of space separated the terrace from the back wall of the hotel. The earth rose steeply from the ground floor of the hotel, creating a deep gap at least twelve or thirteen feet deep between the terrace and the hotel.

The chaise lounges had been facing the mountain, so I pivoted and stood with my back to the hotel. The glare from the snow cut like a blade across my vision. I shaded my eyes and looked up to the brilliant blue of the sky, then I tilted my head back farther until the dark eaves came into sight, black against the azure of the sky. The remaining icicles hung like claws, but under the intensity of the sun, they were melting. I turned back to the gap between the terrace and the hotel.

The snow on the ground didn't look as deep as the surrounding area, but it was as smooth as the sheets on a freshly made bed, except for a single meandering trail— tiny imprints of some small woodland creature—and a narrow indentation an inch or so deep, created as drops from the melting icicles plopped into the snow.

I walked to the far end of the deck and turned back to study the hotel. Vogel was right. Each balcony railing had a mound of snow that was undisturbed. A layer of white covered the roof like a flawless sweep of icing on a cake. I turned and looked up at the mountain slope that stretched up to the toboggan run. The snow on the incline was smooth and unmarred as it ran down to the terrace and then continued on its descent, wrapping around the hotel on my left. I moved to the right side of the terrace.

Beyond the handrail was a steep drop of about twenty feet to a lane that curved up the mountain and disappeared after bending into the trees. Scattered rooftops poked through the pines at higher elevations above the visible strip of the road.

A stone retaining wall enclosed the escarpment. It ran straight up, and the supports for the terrace rested on the top of the wall. Someone with mountaineering experience could have scaled the wall—and there were certainly loads of climbers in St. Moritz—but they couldn't have crossed the terrace to Mrs. Lavington without leaving a trail of footprints. And they couldn't have pulled that trick of walking in a set of already-existing footprints to camouflage their presence. Mrs. Lavington had arrived using the bridge, which was on the other side of the terrace.

Vogel was right. There was no sign that anyone else had been on the terrace except Mrs. Lavington. I should have been able to move on and enjoy my holiday. It was what the average person would do—leave it with the police and turn to skating, skiing, and snowshoeing without giving it another thought, except for a fleeting murmur of commiseration when Mrs. Lavington's name was mentioned. But I couldn't release that tiny quibble of worry that poked at me—especially not after what I'd just observed.

As I kicked the snow from my boots before entering the hotel, I let out a little huff of laughter at myself. A typical holidayer wouldn't have gotten involved in the situation at all, much less be mulling over if the police had it wrong. But, then again, I wasn't exactly conventional.

Skaters, skiers, climbers, and toboggan enthusiasts— tobogganists?—mingled in the lobby, toting their gear or stacking it by the door for one of the bellboys to carry outside later. I found Jasper in the restaurant. Once we were seated and had ordered, he said, "You don't look at all like you were up half the night. How was your chat with the korporale?"

"Vogel says Mrs. Lavington's death was an accident." I took one of the flaky rolls as I described the conversation and included the barest details about the blackmail in a low voice. "I didn't tell you before because I promised Mrs. Lavington to keep it to myself. But now . . . well, you can see why I had to tell the korporale. Although I doubt Korporale Vogel will pursue the blackmail issue. He said her death was an accident and that was that."

"We shall see. Once the police are involved, secrets have a way of coming out. I'm flattered that you shared the news with me—even if it was after the police."

His smile took any sting out of the words. "I know I can trust you with it," I said. "You're very circumspect."

"So circumspect that no one in high society suspects I'm anything but a snappy dresser." I opened my mouth to protest, but he cut me off. "Which is exactly the way I want it. Good camouflage, don't you know."

The waiter brought my hot cocoa. Once he'd left, Jasper picked up his coffee. "The snippets of conversation you overheard on the train . . . you think the two people were talking about Mrs. Lavington?"

"I can't help but wonder."

"Yes, I agree."

"But you believe me about what I heard. I don't think Korporale Vogel does."

"He may believe you, but he can't let on that he does."

We sat in silence for a few minutes, and then Jasper asked, "What are your plans for today?"

"The sun is out, so I suppose I will try snowshoeing. Perhaps with Miss Ravenna and Mr. Vandenberg."

"I'll be closeted in my room today. I hope to finish my project soon." For the remainder of the meal, we discussed various outings and activities, both of us stepping back from the topic of Mrs. Lavington's death.

After the waiter cleared our plates, I said, "I'll let you get to your project," and inched my chair back. Jasper reached across the table and caught my hand. "Do be careful today."

I squeezed his hand. "Today and every day, of course." He made a harumph sound, and I said, "I assure you I intend to focus solely on snowshoeing this morning."

"Of course you do, old bean. Of course. I completely believe those assurances. It's so in keeping with your retiring nature." He gave me a knowing look and kissed my cheek. He lingered a moment, his face close to mine. "Do send for me if you get into a sticky wicket."

I patted his arm. "No sticky wickets this morning, I promise. I'll see you at luncheon."

I found that I quite liked snowshoeing. The air had a crystalline quality to it, so sharp and clean that it almost hurt to breathe in. Miss Ravenna had convinced me to come along with her and Mr. Vandenberg, and we set out around the lake, moving between the towering evergreens robed in snow with the peaks of the Alps as a background.

One wouldn't think walking would require much effort, but I found that as the time went, on I was perspiring, and my breath was coming in short bursts of white puffs. It was hard going, but I settled into a stride that wasn't too demanding and shut down the questions about Mrs. Lavington that were swirling through my thoughts, focusing only on my steps and the natural beauty around me.

We returned to the hotel, and Miss Ravenna and Mr. Vandenberg went off to pack because they were departing on a short tour of the Lower Engadine Valley and would be away for two nights. I had that rather self-satisfied feeling of accomplishment that comes after physical exertion and the successful completion of a task, even if was only a trek along a snowy trail by a lake. Jasper had left a message for me at the front desk. He was at a critical point and had decided to work through luncheon. He would see me for dinner.

I returned my room to change because my wool socks were snow-encrusted, but I realized I had left my gloves downstairs at the front desk when I picked up the message. I was reaching to open the door when a soft *whoosh* sounded, and an envelope was shoved under my door.

I snatched it up and opened the door. The corridor was empty, but a woman was disappearing into a room down the hall. I only caught a glimpse of brown hair and a flash of black dress.

I closed my door and headed for the recently closed door, opening the unsealed envelope as I went.

CHAPTER 14

*T*he envelope was hotel stationery with the name *Alpine House* printed on it. It contained only a scrap of paper that was charred on one side as if it had been snatched out of a fire. The top of the note had burned away, but a portion of the last line was visible. It read, *—ring £10 to the terrace.*

It looked as if Mrs. Lavington *had* been on the terrace to pay off her blackmailer.

I knocked on the door where I'd seen a flash of black skirt disappear. A plump middle-aged woman with pale brown hair threaded through with gray answered. It was the woman Mrs. Lavington had snapped at in the lobby on the day we'd arrived. Her bun was pulled tight, with no wisps of hair escaping it, and she wore a black skirt with a matching cardigan and a plain white blouse underneath. Her startled look flashed over me, then her gaze darted to the hallway behind me.

It appeared she wasn't overcome with grief about her

employer's death. Her skin wasn't blotchy from crying, and her eyes weren't the least bit puffy or pink.

"Hello. You must be Mrs. Lavington's lady's maid?"

She nodded reluctantly. "I'm Etta Morgan, miss." Her hand tightened on the doorknob as if she'd like to close it in my face, but her manners were better than that.

I lifted the burnt paper, and the rosy color drained from her cheeks. "You pushed this under my door."

She picked at the side seam of her skirt in a nervous movement with her free hand. "Begging your pardon, miss, but I didn't know what else to do with it."

"What do you mean?"

"Mrs. Lavington threw it in the fire last night along with the envelope it came in. She tossed them both in. The envelope burned up, but that scrap of paper fell out onto the hearth. Mrs. Lavington didn't notice. She was on her way to dinner and just tossed them both in and walked away, impatient like. She was careless like that. She didn't see things through." She smoothed her hand across the sweep of her hair as if to tuck in a wayward strand, but her coiffure was perfectly in place. "With everything that's happened, I couldn't throw it away. Someone should know."

My room didn't have a fire, and from what I could see of Etta's, she didn't have one either, but I imagined that the room the Lavingtons were staying in was one of the more luxurious accommodations where a fireplace could be part of the alpine decor.

"But why did you bring it to me?"

"Because she talked to you on the train, and you're a lady detective. You'd know what to do with it."

I put on my most persuasive smile and held out the

scorched paper. "I'm afraid I can't do anything with it. What *you* should do is take it to the police."

She shuffled back a step, and her voice, which had been soft and obsequious, quavered. "Go to the police in foreign parts? Please, miss, a woman of my station *cannot* get involved with the police. I'm returning to England as soon as possible. I mustn't have anything to do with that." She gave a sharp nod toward the paper, then looked at the floor, receding after her short burst of firmness back to her meek stance.

"I can see you're quite distressed. Let's sit down and discuss this for a moment. Standing in the corridor is bound to draw attention when someone comes along, which is the last thing you'd want."

Her lips pursed together, the internal debate visible on her face, but then she opened the door wider. She would rather have refused but because of our relative positions in the social strata, she complied.

The room was much smaller than mine and finished more simply, but it was warmer than the hallway. The snow on my socks was melting, and a distinctly unpleasant chilliness had settled around my ankles and feet.

Etta motioned me to the single straight-back chair positioned by a small table while she went to perch on the bed. She picked up a day dress from the bed, careful to avoid a row of pins. She folded her mending loosely and put it beside an open sewing box.

I set the charred paper and the envelope on the little table between us. "Let me start off by introducing myself properly. I'm Olive Belgrave."

A smile flickered for a moment. Color was coming back into Etta's face. When she wasn't distressed and frowning, she was rather pretty, with her creamy rose-tinted complexion and her brown eyes that were fringed with dark lashes. "Pleased to make your acquaintance."

I touched the corner of the paper that hadn't been singed. "You recognize the significance of this note." She must understand, otherwise she would have tossed it back in the fire instead of saving it.

She answered promptly. "That Mrs. Lavington was being blackmailed? Yes." Now that the door was closed, her strained manner fell away and her shoulders relaxed.

I wasn't at all surprised that she was aware of the blackmail. It was difficult to keep secrets from servants, especially from one's maid. "She'd received this type of note before?"

"A few times. Maybe three before this one?" Her flat dark brows pinched together as she thought. "Yes, three others that I know of. Mrs. Lavington was in a state with the first one. Frightfully agitated, she was. That was near Christmas. The next time was in the spring. I remember because I was changing out her dresses in the wardrobe, putting away her new summer frocks and evening gowns. I'd gone downstairs to fetch a bit of ironing, and when I returned, Mrs. Lavington was tossing a note into the fire. I acted like I hadn't seen her. She didn't mention it, so I certainly didn't say anything about it."

"And it happened a third time?"

"Yes, miss, before the midsummer ball. The note was with the post. The letters she received usually came in handwritten envelopes. Only those were typed." She pointed at the paper with the blackened edge. "I brought it with her breakfast tray. Later, when I returned for the tray, the smell of smoke was in the air and there were ashes in the fireplace. I cleaned it up myself instead of calling for one of the housemaids. I could tell Mrs. Lavington wanted to keep the notes a secret."

"I see." And I did. Etta didn't want to take the risk of word getting out that her mistress was burning paper in the fireplace during the summer, which might have happened if she'd called for someone else to clean up the mess. Mrs. Lavington might have thought Etta was gossiping about her. "Mrs. Lavington never spoke about them?"

"Not directly. After the second and third note, she did make little comments—as if she were talking to herself instead of to me—about the despicable nature of people, that they were demanding and grasping, and that it wasn't right."

Etta's information tallied with Mrs. Lavington's account. It appeared Mrs. Lavington had been honest with me about the notes themselves. Now that she'd begun talking, Etta's earlier reticence had dropped away, and she broke the quiet in the room as she continued, "I think Mrs. Lavington pawned some jewelry too. A cameo brooch and a string of black pearls. She said she lost them during a house party, but I saw her coming out of Stoad & Hood. It was my afternoon off."

"Is that a pawnbroker?" I asked, not familiar with the name.

"I didn't linger reading the fine print of the sign, but I assume so. There were three gold balls over the door. I turned around and hurried away so she wouldn't see me."

My mind boggled at the thought of Mrs. Lavington at a pawnbroker, but if she didn't want to tell her husband about the blackmail, it might have been her only way to raise money. She certainly couldn't have withdrawn money from a joint bank account without him becoming aware of it. "Do you have any idea who sent the notes to her?"

"No."

"Was there anyone who was upset with her?"

"That would be many people, miss." Etta dipped her head again and looked at the floor, her open manner shutting down.

"Etta, whatever details you can share would be helpful."

Head still down, she looked up at me, her face troubled, then she gave a jerky nod. "Mrs. Lavington had a way of putting people's backs up with little comments. Spiky, they were. I think she actually enjoyed riling people up. And she was very demanding. She expected everything to be perfect—the estate, her clothing, travel arrangements. Everything, really."

"Does anyone stand out in your memory?" The blackmail had been going on for months, so I added, "Any long-standing animosity?"

"Mrs. Lavington and her friend Mrs. Grogan were always arguing. I suppose she argued with Mrs. Grogan the most often. They'd go at it hammer and tongs sometimes."

"What did they disagree about?"

Etta plucked at some lint on her skirt and kept her

attention on the fabric as she said, "It was always about the millinery. Round and round, they'd go. Mrs. Grogan wanted to buy out Mrs. Lavington, but Mrs. Lavington said she'd never sell."

"Anyone else? Did she argue with Mr. Lavington?"

"No, they were fond of each other. They did spend a lot of time apart—perhaps that's why they got on. Him with his mountain climbing and her with her social engagements, but when they were both at home, there were no fights that I remember."

She was quiet a moment, then added, "I worked for Mrs. Lavington for many years. There was talk when I first arrived about an older woman who accused Mrs. Lavington of doing something terrible, but I don't know the details. Something about a party, but it was hushed up. The staff was forbidden to talk about it. Of course, some people dropped little hints, but I never got the full story."

"I see. Well, it sounds as if this should certainly be handed off to Korporale Vogel. He should see it and hear what you have to say." I pushed the note across the table toward her.

She drew back, scooting away like a mouse scurrying away from a cat. An amiable atmosphere had developed between us, but the fragile bubble of affinity popped like a soap bubble. "No, I could never do that. I told you everything. You're a lady detective. You can tell them everything I said but without telling them it was me who told you. I cannot be associated with the police."

I tried to convince her, but deep down I knew I wouldn't be able to budge her. And I didn't blame her. Etta's employer had died. She needed a new job, and she couldn't afford to have even a hint of scandal associated with her. Going to the police would certainly fall into the *scandalous* category, even if she was only passing on evidence. That action could cause future job prospects to dry up.

"Please, miss." She pointed to the note. "Take it with you and keep my name out of it." I hesitated, and she licked her lips, then spoke in a rush. "If you leave it, I'll have to tear it up. I'm sorry, but that's the truth."

She was probably being completely honest. She didn't want to speak to the police, and she wouldn't leave the note to be found by someone else. "I'm sorry you're in this situation. I understand why you don't want to come forward." I picked up the scorched paper. "I'll do as you ask, but if anything changes—if it's discovered that Mrs. Lavington's death wasn't an accident—you may have to speak to the police."

"Thank you, miss." Relief flowed through her words, and I was sure she'd completely glossed over my caveat. Etta closed the door behind me, and I imagined she didn't waste a moment before pulling out her luggage to begin packing. The Swiss police would find it difficult to speak to her if she wasn't in the country.

I returned to my room. I was sorry Etta was in an awkward spot. I was also sorry that I'd have to bother Korporale Vogel again. I was sure he'd be delighted to see me.

CHAPTER 15

I returned to my room, stripped off my cold, sodden socks, and put on a fresh pair. Even though my room was warm, I felt chilled and took up the quilt from the end of the bed. I wrapped it around me like a cloak as I sat down at the desk. I took out a sheet of hotel stationery, then stared at the ceiling a moment before I picked up my pen.

Dear Korporale Vogel,

The enclosed item came into my possession today. It was slipped under my door. I thought it should be passed along to you. Unfortunately, I can't provide any more details about it.

Sincerely,
Olive Belgrave

I sat back and read over it, then gave a little nod of satisfaction. Well, that would do . . . for now. It was the truth—not the whole truth, but I'd managed to keep my promise to Etta that I wouldn't mention her.

Before I sealed it up, I took the typed note over to the window and studied it in the light. I certainly wasn't an expert in analyzing documents, but it was easy to see that the pound sign wasn't sitting evenly on the line. It tilted slightly to the left. And there must have been a little scratch on the zero key of the typewriter. It wasn't a full oval. A thin line cut through it on the bottom right-hand side.

I put the remains of the charred note in an envelope along with my letter, sealed it, and addressed it to the korporale. I dropped it off at the front desk. The attendant said Vogel was in the hotel, and it would be handed off immediately. I decided it would be a good time to visit the shops.

I dashed upstairs, retrieved my coat, and then walked down the steeply descending streets to the center of town. I strolled along, admiring cuckoo clocks, souvenir spoons, and postcards. As I trudged up an incline of one of the lanes, I could feel that I was becoming acclimated to the alpine altitude. My breathing wasn't as labored as it had been yesterday.

I paused outside a boutique, admiring full-length fur coats and exquisite evening gowns. I refrained from going inside, though. My income was much better than it had been a few months before, but it certainly didn't run to mink coats. I bought some postcards at another shop, then continued on my way, dipping in and out of the shops. I was considering a gilded cuckoo clock with not one, but two—two!—cherubs that flitted out on the hour. Would it make a good wedding present for my cousin Gwen? It was gloriously excessive. I thought she would appreciate the absurdity of it, but I wasn't sure if my future cousin-in-law, Inspector Longly, would.

"Olive?"

I turned and found Juliet standing in the aisle, a St. Moritz souvenir spoon in her hand. "For my friend, who collects them." She pointed the spoon at the clock I'd been considering. "Are you purchasing it?"

"It would make quite a statement, wouldn't it? But no, it's not quite what I'm looking for." I joined her, moving along the aisle toward the cash register. "How are you feeling? No ill effects from the fire?"

She held out her arm and twisted it this way and that. "Perfectly fine. It was frightening, but no damage done, thank goodness."

"I'm glad to hear it."

"And you've heard about Emmaline, I suppose? Everyone is talking about it," Juliet said as we rounded a rack of postcards. Her face transformed to a grave expression, but like Etta, her eyes showed no sign of recent tears. "Very sad news." She delivered the statement as if she were talking about a picnic being called off because of rain.

I agreed but didn't say anything about seeing Mrs. Lavington's body on the terrace. Juliet leaned in and said in an excited whisper, "Are you investigating? I know it's ghastly of me to ask, but I can't help it."

I stopped and turned toward her. "Investigating? No, of course not."

"But why not? You're the lady detective."

"The police say her death was an accident." That was the official line, and while I might speculate with Jasper, I wasn't about to do the same with Juliet.

She examined a key chain with an image of the lake and mountains on it, then picked up a snow globe that contained a replica of St. Moritz with tiny clock towers, the lake, and surrounding mountains. Juliet picked up another globe, turned it upside down and replaced it on the shelf. As the tiny white flakes drifted down through the liquid, she said, "Well, I think it's most odd—to die after an icicle hits you." She looked at me out of the corner of her eye. "It would bear looking into, I'd think. The chances of that happening are—"

"Rare, I've heard."

She pulled another key chain out for a look, then released it. It clattered against the others. "But when it's someone like Emmaline, it does make one wonder."

"What do you mean?"

The clocks, which were mounted on all four walls of the shop, began chiming. It was the top of the hour, and a cavalcade of cuckooing broke out all around us. Figurines danced, hammers struck anvils, birds flitted in and out of little doors.

Juliet raised her voice. "There's a nice little restaurant around the corner where I planned to get tea and some cakes. Care to join me?"

I agreed, and once we were seated across from each other in one of the high-backed wooden booths that ringed the restaurant, with a teapot between us and some delicious rolls and cakes, Juliet said, "If you want to dance the polka, come here in the evening. The beefsteak is good too."

"You know St. Moritz quite well?"

"Oh yes. I spend most of my time here except for the holidays. With the Cresta Run, St. Moritz is the center of the sporting set in the winter. And the summer season is nearly as popular." She stirred sugar into her tea. "But that's not why I wanted to talk to you. You're *truly* not looking into Emmaline's death?"

"No. It was an accident."

"Was it? Was it really?"

I still didn't want to share any of my questions about the death with Juliet, so I asked, "Why did you think I was looking into it?"

Juliet sighed and studied the cheerful red curtains on either side of the window above our booth. "I realize this will sound catty, but Emmaline constantly made people angry. And I don't mean angry in a frustrated or annoyed way. I mean vilely angry."

"You think someone was upset with her? Upset enough to kill her?"

Juliet put the spoon in the saucer and picked up her tea. "If someone's livelihood was at stake, then yes, I think it's possible. Someone like Hattie."

"Hattie Grogan? But doesn't her husband work at a bank?" I was fairly sure I'd heard her mention it in the dining car on the train.

"In a junior position. Rob's family was quite affluent before the war, but now they're rather strained. Rob and Hattie seem to live as if unlimited funds are still available. They have a divine flat in London. I can't think how they afford it. It must be the hats that pay the rent—and buy the tickets to the Alps." Juliet leaned over the table. "Hattie was here on a campaign to convince Emmaline to sell her portion of the business to her."

"Yes, you mentioned that before. But how could Hattie buy her out if they're struggling financially?"

"I heard Hattie and Rob arguing yesterday at breakfast. Apparently, Hattie had convinced a relative—her father, I think—to lend Hattie the money to buy out Emmaline. She and Rob were arguing about how much they'd have to offer to tempt Emmaline to sell. It sounded as if Rob wanted to pay her the exact amount Emmaline had put up for the lease on the shop, but Hattie said they should offer more because"—her voice changed to an imitation of Hattie's less sophisticated accent as she said—"*no price was too high* to get her out of the business." She returned to her normal speaking voice. "Apparently, Emmaline was running the shop into the ground. Hattie said that if they wanted to survive, she had to get Emmaline out. The cost didn't matter. At one point, Hattie even said, *She has to go.* Those were her exact words. I heard her."

"It sounds rather awkward for them, but not something that usually means murder."

"Oh, it was indeed awkward. And everyone knows Hattie did all the *real* work at the shop. It's her creations that sell. All Emmaline did was put up the money for the lease and get the word out among the posh set that LaRue's was the place for hats. I suppose it would have worked if Emmaline had stayed out of the day-to-day running of the shop, but apparently Emmaline liked to dabble, which caused problems."

"I'm sure business partners often have disagreements, but very few resort to something as drastic as . . ."

I didn't want to actually say the word, but Juliet jumped in.

"Murder? Yes, I know. But if there were anyone who would be a candidate for murder, it would be Emmaline." She began ticking names off on her fingers. "Hattie, Rob, Mrs. Ashford, and who knows how many of her staff and servants would like to see—"

"Mrs. Ashford?" I interrupted, surprised.

Juliet dropped her hands to her lap. "I admit that's pure speculation on my part. But Mrs. Ashford was adamant that Emmaline not be invited to join any of the ladies' sports activities or committees. She's the only person Mrs. Ashford has blackballed. Not that Emmaline would have been interested. She detested outdoor activities and sport of any kind."

Juliet tapped the table to emphasize her next point. "And anytime Emmaline was mentioned, Mrs. Ashford went quiet and frowned in that way she does when she's angry. Mrs. Ashford is very circumspect. She never says anything critical or speaks badly of anyone, but I can tell when she's upset. Something happened between Mrs. Ashford and Emmaline, something very bad indeed for Mrs. Ashford to react in that way. She's normally the kindest of souls." Juliet poured more tea into her cup. "As you can see, the list of people who weren't happy with Emmaline is quite extensive."

"What about you? Would you be on that list too?" I'd sensed a tension between the two women on the train. The flare of animosity had been evident, and Juliet was doing her best to paint Emmaline in a very unflattering light, to say the least.

Juliet made a face that often accompanied the words *don't be silly*. "Emmaline was . . . tedious. She didn't want anything to do with sport and thought my work to promote ladies' athletics was absurd. But that was Emmaline all over. If she didn't see the point in a thing, there was no need for it. She couldn't see outside her own perspective. No sympathy, you know. Or allowance for interests and attitudes that didn't match hers. Just because she was delicate and couldn't participate in skiing and skating didn't mean those things weren't worthwhile." Juliet picked up her cup and looked at me over the rim. "But other people had much more at stake than a difference of opinion about sporting activities. Can you see why I doubt it was an accident? Now you must tell me, have you found out anything else about her death?"

"No," I said with a laugh. "I'm simply here to enjoy the Alps. Not to investigate anything."

Her lips pushed into a pout. "Well, that is disappointing. I don't believe that you're not looking into it for a moment." She gave a little shake of her head. "I know I must seem the most terrible ghoul, asking all these questions and listing possible suspects. I can't help myself. You have to understand that Emmaline and I were chums when we were younger, but we lost touch. For many years, we've been acquaintances, not close friends. I do find details around things of this sort rather fascinating. I'm actually a tremendous fan of crime fiction. I just read *The Red House Mystery*. Do you know it? The author is A. A. Milne."

"No, I haven't. I believe Jasper mentioned he had a copy of it. I'll have to ask if he brought it along."

"Where is Mr. Rimington? I haven't seen him at all. I thought he would be on the toboggan run today. All the chaps seemed to want to conquer the Cresta Run right away."

"I'm sure he'll be taking a turn on the Cresta soon."

We spent the rest of our time talking about books. As we pulled on our coats, Juliet asked, "Have you given skiing a try yet?"

"I've barely had time to skate."

"Then you must come with me. Will you give it a go? We'll only go to the small hills. Nothing too terrifying, I promise."

I agreed and slid out of the booth. "Brilliant," she said, but my attention was drawn to another booth as we passed it. Juliet continued speaking, saying something about her schedule, then her tone sharpened. "Olive?"

"What?" I pulled my attention back to her.

"Tomorrow afternoon?"

"Oh yes. That's fine. I think I left my package of post-cards in the booth. You go on. I don't want to hold you up. See you tomorrow."

Juliet left, and even though my postcards were tucked away in my coat pocket, I went back to our table. It gave me the opportunity to study a man and woman who were sitting side by side in one of the booths. I'd been wrong about Etta. She hadn't packed up and departed. She was talking animatedly with a man who looked familiar. Their hands were clasped together on the table.

Without his top hat and the double rows of shining buttons on his coat, it took me a moment to place him. Etta and Mr. Klein were a couple?

I didn't want to draw attention to myself, so I kept up my pace as I passed their table, but I needn't have worried. They didn't look away from each other as I went by them on the way out. I doubted anything less than someone opening a Christmas cracker beside them would have pulled their attention away from each other.

CHAPTER 16

I returned to the hotel, and as I was walking across the lobby, Vogel fell into step beside me. My heart sank. I'd hoped to avoid speaking to him and put off any questions about the note I'd sent him for at least a few more hours. It would be tricky to keep my promise to Etta and also not lie to him.

"Good afternoon, Miss Belgrave. Do you have a moment?"

"Of course."

"So kind of you." He led the way across the lobby to the area behind the front desk. "The hotel proprietor has kindly extended the use of his office to me again today." He gestured for me to proceed him into the small room. He closed the door and moved behind the desk. I took off my coat and folded it across my lap as I took a seat in the chair across from him.

Vogel pushed a heap of papers and folders to the side of the desk. "Would you like a cup of tea? Or perhaps coffee?"

"No, thank you." I decided to plunge right in and get the worst of it over right away. "You received the envelope I left for you?"

"Yes, I have it here." He tapped the top folder on the stack. His manner was different from last evening. Instead of tired and reserved, he seemed to be brimming with energy, but I suppose few people are at their best in the middle of the night. "We'll come to that later. First, I must tell you that when I heard your name, it was familiar to me, but I wasn't able to place it until today. We have a mutual acquaintance: Mr. Hightower."

"The publisher of Hightower Books?"

Vogel angled his chair to the side and crossed one leg over the other. "Exactly. He's the father of an old friend of mine. My father was English, and I spent quite a few years at a boarding school in England, where I met Rodger Hightower. Vernon is his father. I often stayed at the Hightower home during the holidays when I couldn't travel to my own family. I've continued my friendship with the family, and when I visit England, I do my best to dine with Rodger. Last year Rodger invited me to dinner with his wife and his parents. Vernon mentioned a young woman he'd hired to sort out a problem with one of his authors who had gone missing."

I certainly hadn't expected to have a conversation about my time at Blackburn Hall. "Yes, that was a most intriguing case."

"I also spoke to Inspector Longly. In short, Miss Belgrave, you have excellent references. *And* you have a knack for figuring out what is going on below the surface."

"Thank you." I couldn't quite keep the slight inflection

out of my voice, which gave the words the sound of a question. The korporale sounded . . . almost complimentary, which hardly ever—never?—happened when I had discussions with police officials.

He smiled. "Not many people have such a talent." He sat forward and clasped his hands together on the desk. "Miss Belgrave, you think the death of Mrs. Lavington has the appearance of an accident but is certainly suspicious and, possibly, not an accident, but murder."

I felt myself blink at the bald statement. "Yes," I agreed. "As I suggested last evening, that's my instinct, but I have no proof to support that idea."

Vogel thumped his knuckles on the desk. "Exactly. *That* is the problem. And I think you may be the person to help me solve it."

"I'm not sure I follow." Vogel's change in manner puzzled me. I felt off-balance, as if I were trying to find my footing on a ship in turbulent water. "When we last spoke, you were adamant that Mrs. Lavington's death was an accident."

"That was last night. I wasn't able to fully examine the terrace until after photographs had been taken and the doctor had finished. Once Mrs. Lavington's body was removed and I could return to the terrace—well, let me just say my perspective has changed. Quite a few intriguing things have come to light that indicate Mrs. Lavington's death was *not* an accident. However, I have no physical evidence to prove a crime was committed, nor can I link anyone to the terrace last night except Mrs. Lavington. Rather, I have evidence of a negative sort. But let us slow down." He took out a notebook and placed it on the folder. "I assume you've visited the terrace since the accident?" At my nod, he continued speaking as he flipped pages. "And I'm sure you didn't fail to notice the eaves."

What sort of strangeness was this that the police discussed evidence with me? Was I Alice down the rabbit hole? "Yes," I said cautiously.

"And I assume you noted something rather interesting about them?"

"I did." I hesitated. He'd been so dismissive last night. Was this some sort of trick, a strange sort of interrogation method that would mire me in suspicion? But as he took up a pen, he nodded at me to go on, his expression expectant, like a teacher encouraging a student who had the correct answer to speak up. I plunged in. "The edge of the eaves, while deep, doesn't extend completely over the terrace."

"Yes, that's it exactly." He pointed the pen at me to punctuate his words. "Which means an icicle could not have fallen directly on Mrs. Lavington. I believe Mrs. Lavington's death was staged to look as if an icicle killed her. However, I have no link to anyone who could have committed the crime."

He placed the pen in the gutter of the notebook, which was filled with small spare strokes. He must have taken his own notes on the witnesses from last evening. "Miss Belgrave, you know these people. You traveled with them on the train. You're mingling with them here at the hotel and participating in the winter sports they pursue. Might you consider coming on board the investigation in a consultancy role?"

I was stunned.

He must have taken my silence as offense because he

hurried on. "I'm afraid it would be an unpaid position. Our resources are stretched as they are, but I thought perhaps your personal interest might convince you to collaborate with me?"

Had I heard him correctly? I measured my words as I spoke. "You're inviting me to become part of the official investigation? Me?"

"Yes, you, Miss Belgrave."

Perhaps his English wasn't quite as good as I thought. Had he gotten the wrong end of the stick? "But I'm not associated with the police. I just help people sort out delicate problems."

He waved a hand, swatting away my caution. "I have a family friend who vouches for your integrity as well as the recommendation of an inspector from the Yard. Surely that is enough? Not to mention that you've been instrumental in solving several crimes and have worked closely with the police to do so. As I said, you have an entrée into the lives of these people that I, as a police official, will never have."

"Well, I'm flattered, of course, but what about your doubt about the blackmail? Last evening you seemed rather dismissive of that detail."

"Ah, but now we have proof of it, which puts a different complexion on things. And I have my negative proof, as I call it . . ." He sat back and spread his hands. "It is a different situation now, no?"

"But *I* could have typed that note."

"Do you travel with a typewriter, Miss Belgrave?"

"No."

"And do you have access to a typewriter?"

"No."

"The only typewriter in the hotel belongs to Mr. Hoffman's secretary. He and the front desk staff have confirmed that no one has used it in the last two days except Mr. Hoffman's secretary."

"I see your point, but a guest—"

"The bellboys and maids have confirmed none of the guests in the hotel have a typewriter."

I couldn't help but smile. "You've been quite meticulous." My worry about Vogel turning the tables and switching from accommodating to suspicious was fading. Instead, this exchange felt more like a friendly game of tennis with us lobbing the ball back and forth. It was my turn. "Perhaps I brought the typed note with me."

He raised a finger as if I'd made a good point, then said, "But you did not meet Mrs. Lavington until you were on the train—that I have confirmed." He'd won his point and leaned forward. "You see why I believe I can take you into my confidence." He paused and tilted his head to the side, a wrinkle creasing a line between his brows as his tone turned uncertain. "You are extremely quiet, Miss Belgrave. Perhaps you'd rather enjoy your holiday and not bother with solving a seemingly impossible crime."

I shook off my stunned bemusement and sat straighter. "Thank you for the invitation. I'm interested, Korporale Vogel—very interested. I only hesitated because I've never found the inspectors in England to be as open to—ah—collaboration, as you call it."

He let out a little laugh. "You will find that we are often forward-thinking on the Continent. I'm happy to have your agreement. Excellent! Now, to work. I have spent the morning interviewing people who were in the lounge last evening to establish the movements of everyone. You, along with your party, which consisted of"—he consulted his notebook—"Mr. Jasper Rimington, Miss Bebe Ravenna, and Mr. Vandenberg. The four of you did not leave the lounge after Mrs. Lavington departed. The doctor believes Mrs. Lavington died quite soon after leaving the lounge, which occurred at ten till ten. You did not leave the lounge until the aftermath of the fire had been sorted out at after eleven. You are *in the clear*, as they say in the films."

"Well, that's good to know." I was glad he didn't suspect any of my group from last night. It was a relief that he didn't expect me to spy on Jasper, Miss Ravenna, or Mr. Vandenberg—that could have been rather awkward.

"Now," Vogel adjusted the notebook, aligning it with the edge of the desk as he continued, "you reported yesterday that Mrs. Lavington was being blackmailed—something her husband says he knew nothing about, by the way. I met with him briefly about half an hour ago. It's fortuitous that I received your letter before I spoke to him because I was able to ask him about that detail."

"He had no suspicion at all?"

"None. I believe he was telling the truth. The news . . . what is the English saying? . . . knocked him at sevens?"

"Knocked him for six."

He repeated the phrase as if he was memorizing the idiom for future use. "You must forgive me, I sometimes forget these delightful expressions I learned years ago."

"How is Mr. Lavington holding up?"

Vogel flicked up his fingers and hitched up one

shoulder in a gesture that I translated to mean, *What do you expect?* "He had the look of the shell-shocked. I found him in his room with the drapes drawn. He was sitting in the dark, smoking, and had apparently been at it all night. The ashtray beside him was full. He was unshaven and still in his evening clothes. He answered my questions readily enough, but he was . . . struggling to take in the events of last night. And when I asked him about the blackmail, he looked absolutely stunned. I told him to attempt to get some sleep."

To lose your wife in such an unexpected way and then learn she was also being blackmailed would certainly be one shock after another—unless he was one of the people I'd overheard whispering on the train. "So you don't regard him as a suspect?"

"On the contrary, he's the top suspect. It's his wife who's dead. The closest family members always go under the microscope. I only mean to say that he appears to be quite broken up. We'll come back to Mr. Lavington. I'd like to consider the blackmail for the moment. The question remains, why would a blackmailer do away with the source of their income?"

"Well, if Mrs. Lavington told me the truth about the amounts, the sums of money were fairly small—in comparison to what might have been asked. I'd think the Lavingtons would be viewed as fairly well-off."

"Yes, Mrs. Lavington would appear to be a rich target." He paused to smile briefly at the pun, then said, "I'll send off an inquiry today to their bank."

I wrestled with the thought of telling him about Etta's sighting of Mrs. Lavington emerging from a pawnbroker. If I mentioned it, he'd surely want to know who told me.

While I was still struggling to come up with a way to reveal the information while shielding Etta, Vogel continued, "And then there is the detail of the conversation you overheard on the train. The fact that Mrs. Lavington died shortly after the tête-à-tête is suggestive, but not proof her death was murder. However, we'll keep these details in mind. For now, I intend to focus specifically on Mrs. Lavington's death. I feel that area is where we can make the most headway in discovering proof of a criminal act."

Vogel turned to a different page in his notebook. "As I mentioned earlier, instances of injuries and even death related to icicles are not unknown. However, they typically happen when the sun is out, and the icicles are melting, not on a cold snowy evening with the temperature dropping. Perhaps you also noticed that someone broke the icicles off the eaves to make it look as if one of them struck Mrs. Lavington?"

"Yes, I saw there were several gaps in the line of icicles on the eaves," I said. "Surely that narrows down the suspect pool to people who had access to the upper floors at the back of the hotel?"

"Unfortunately, the middle room on the top floor was unoccupied. The chambermaid found it unlocked this morning. I don't want to alarm you, but the locks here, as in many hotels, are not incredibly secure. We've never had a problem with robbery. In fact, many guests leave their rooms unlocked."

"So it wouldn't be difficult for someone to enter the middle guest room on the top floor and knock down the icicles."

"Correct, but it would require some sort of implement to reach the icicles because the eaves are not within arm's

129

length. And that detail provides the only physical evidence to indicate something is very wrong about Mrs. Lavington's death. Or, rather, the *lack* of evidence points to a careful plan. Once I noticed the missing icicles and the width of the eaves, I had my men search the hotel. The maids store their brooms, mops, and buckets in a cupboard in the hallway, which does not have a lock on it. When examined, my men could find no fingerprints at all on the broom handle. Yet the mop and buckets were covered with them. All the fingerprints found belong to the maids."

"It's a kind of negative proof," I agreed.

He took a single sheet of paper from one of the folders and handed it to me. "This list of names is everyone I've been able to determine who has some connection with Mrs. Lavington. The checks beside certain people indicate those who were in the lounge at some point last evening.

I scanned the list.

√ Ben Lavington - husband
√ Hattie Grogan - friend
√ Rob Grogan - Hattie's husband
X Ignatius Hale - mountaineer; training with Mr. Lavington, met Mrs. Lavington on the train
X Vincent Blinkhorn - mountaineer; training with Mr. Lavington, met Mrs. Lavington on the train
√ Amy Ashford – acquaintance; traveled on the train with Mrs. Lavington
√ Juliet Lenox - distant friend
Etta Morgan - maid
√ Olive Belgrave - met on the train

130

√ Jasper Rimington - acquaintance

√ Bebe Ravenna - no relationship; present in the lounge

√ Evert Vandenberg - no relationship; present in the lounge

"Why do you have an *X* beside the names of Mr. Hale and Mr. Blinkhorn?"

"They were at the bar in the Koller restaurant during the time I'm interested in. In fact, they didn't return to the hotel until after midnight, and they were quite drunk."

"Yes, I saw them arrive while I was in the lobby, but I didn't realize they'd been gone the whole time."

"They definitely were. Several reliable witnesses state the cousins were at the Koller from half-past nine until a quarter to midnight. Word is that they were very taken with several beautiful fräulein who were also there."

"Mr. Hale and Mr. Blinkhorn are cousins, then? I'd wondered. They look so much alike."

"Almost like twins," Vogel agreed. "But Blinkhorn has a —what is the word?" He pointed to his chin. "Dent?—in his chin."

"Oh, a dimple. I hadn't noticed that."

"A dimple, yes. It's the only discernible difference I could see."

He nodded at the list and asked, "Have I missed anyone who knew Mrs. Lavington?"

I handed it back to him. "The only person that I can think you might need to add is the doorman."

"The doorman?"

"Yes, when I arrived at the hotel, the doorman looked at Mrs. Lavington with—well, the only way I can describe it is a look of loathing. She seemed completely unaware of it, but he had a visceral reaction when he saw her. He had a reaction of a completely different type when he saw her lady's maid, Etta Morgan. This afternoon, the two of them were in a restaurant where I had tea. They seemed to be a couple."

"Miss Etta Morgan and"—he turned back the pages of his notebook—"Fredrick Klein, head doorman. That detail brings us neatly to the envelope you sent me earlier today. I can't help but think that a person such as a lady's maid would be in an ideal position to find a scrap of paper . . . "

I hadn't been incredibly impressed by the korporale on first meeting him, but my opinion of him was rapidly undergoing a revision. He was much sharper than he seemed. Or perhaps his manner of casual disregard he'd adopted earlier was intended to put people off their guard. In any case, I'd underestimated his acumen. "I promised not to reveal the name of the person."

He nodded, clearly not surprised. "This person is afraid of coming forward, yes? They don't want to jeopardize any future employment. I understand." He drummed the fingers of his left hand on the stack of paper, which made a rustling *rat-tat-a-tat*. "Well, I'll look into the background of those two people and speak to them if necessary."

"And besides inquiring at the bank, you might also check with the pawnbrokers Stoad & Hood. I can't really say more than that—"

Vogel snorted and waved off any further explanation as he picked up his pen. "No need to spell it out, Miss Belgrave.

I suspect I know where the information came from, but I'll merely check on the accuracy of it before speaking to," he cleared his throat, "*anyone* here about it. Don't worry. I'll be circumspect." He tapped the list of names and said with a brisk moving-on tone, "Do you know anything else about these people that could be useful to the investigation?"

"I heard Mr. and Mrs. Grogan were keen to buy out Mrs. Lavington. Mrs. Grogan and Mrs. Lavington were in a joint business venture together, a millinery," I explained. "It's called LaRue's."

He turned back a few pages in his notebook. "Curious," he said dryly. "Neither Mrs. Grogan nor her husband mentioned that. It is details such as these that are helpful. I would have eventually uncovered the business connection, but your input will expedite things. Anything else? No? Then I'll proceed with inquiries about all the individuals through official channels."

"And what would you like me to do?"

"Simply be among these people," he said as he gestured to the list. "Listen and watch. If you discover anything else, please let me know."

"I suppose you'd like me to keep my involvement a secret?"

"By no means. I've already heard questions about whether the lady sleuth is *on the case* of Mrs. Lavington's death—from one of my men, no less," he said with little laugh. "In my experience, denials and obfuscations only fuel speculation. No, feel free to talk about how the befuddled korporale," he put a hand on his chest and bowed his head, "asked for your opinion about the preliminary inquiry into Mrs. Lavington's accident. Make me out to be a buffoon. It can only lull the criminal into a sense of security."

"Of false security, as I've learned today."

"You give me the greatest of compliments, Miss Belgrave. It is a wonderful thing for an investigator to be underestimated. That is when people tend to make mistakes."

CHAPTER 17

I left the office and came out into the lobby, where I found Jasper, Rob and Hattie Grogan, and the two young climbers, Mr. Blinkhorn and Mr. Hale, in a cluster. Jasper said, "Olive, we're off to the Cresta Run. Care to come along?"

Hattie wound her scarf around her neck and pulled gloves out of her pockets. She wore a tight-fitting tangerine-colored knit hat that matched her scarf. "I'm spectating. I have no desire to fly down the horrid ice track. Rob has promised to do nothing excessively daring." She pinned him with the kind of sharp glance a teacher might use to keep a troublemaker in line.

Rob threw up his mittened hands. "I've promised, just an easy slide down the ice. No dangerous speeds."

I was carrying my coat, and I slipped it on. "I'll join you." I wanted to see the famous toboggan run, and, while I might give it a go another time, today I'd stay with Hattie. It would be the perfect opportunity to talk privately with her.

135

We left the hotel and walked a few blocks before turning up a lane that switched back and forth, climbing up the slope. Jasper and I were the last of the group, and we fell back a few steps so that we could speak quietly to each other. "Taking a break from your work?" I asked between huffing breaths. The incline was steep, and after only a few steps I was already winded.

"I found myself at a bit of a block." Jasper's breath clouded the frosty air. "Some brisk mountain air might give me a new perspective. And I can't stay holed up in the room all day every day. People will begin to ask questions."

"They already are. I saw Juliet earlier, and she wanted to know why she hadn't seen you."

"Good thing I'm nearing the end of my project." Jasper squinted at the sky. The sun was already low. Its golden rays sliced through the treetops, casting long shadows across the snow. "I figure we have time for maybe two runs. How has your day been?"

"It's been . . . intriguing. I have much to tell you, but it will have to be later, when we are alone."

"I look forward to it—as I always look forward to time alone with you." He sent me a quick glance that made my cheeks heat despite the cold air.

After that, we saved our breath for the climb. My thighs burned as I took long steps up the gradient toward the Leaning Tower, which was all that remained of a twelfth-century church. Eventually, we rounded a curve in the path, and the crowd around the hut at the top of the run came into sight and then the track itself.

The toboggan run serpentined down the mountain. Its sharpest turns were banked with vertical walls of hard-packed snow and ice, some of them taller than a man.

Rob went off to inform the club the group was here, and I asked Jasper, "Have you seen Mr. Lavington today?"

"No, but he sent a note around yesterday to me to let me know he'd arranged for me to take a run here on the Cresta. He's a member of the St. Moritz Tobogganing Club. Lavington was supposed to climb with Hale and Blinkhorn today, but that had to be canceled, of course. That's why they've come along with us. Lavington has a lot to deal with, arranging transport for his wife's body back to England and so forth."

"Yes, I imagine so." Although with Vogel's concerns around Mrs. Lavington's death, I wondered if the body would be released right away. "Will there be an inquest, I wonder?"

"There might be. I'm not sure how things of this sort are handled in Switzerland. If there is, we'll probably have to be there."

"I'll have to ask Korporale Vogel."

Jasper hitched up an eyebrow. "Having regular meetings with him, are you?"

"Something like that."

"Indeed?"

"Yes, I'll tell you later about a very exciting development. Vogel isn't quite what I thought. Turns out, he's really rather clever."

Jasper didn't respond for a moment. "Well. That's unexpected."

"I know. Exactly what I thought. He's not at all like the inspectors I've dealt with in the past. Very forward-thinking. It's refreshing."

Jasper made an *mm-hmm* noise, his gaze on our group, which was farther up the hill. "Righto. Capital." At that point we caught up with the rest of our group, and I was glad to have a moment to catch my breath. Mr. Hale and Mr. Blinkhorn were there waiting for us, looking practically like mirror images except that their coats were different colors. One of them greeted us heartily, while the other raised a hand in greeting and looked on quietly. I wasn't fast enough to look for the dimple, and I wasn't sure who was who, so I refrained from saying either man's name. They both seemed to be quite recovered from their late night.

There was some back-and-forth, sorting out who would ride with whom and what order they'd go in. The men were informed that, as new riders, they would have to start at the Junction, which was about a third of the way from the top, so we trooped down through the forest. Hattie and I took up a spot at one of the banked turns, a bend of one hundred and eighty degrees, where riders flew by. They swooped up the glossy bank at a nearly perpendicular angle to where our feet were planted on a little tromped-down path behind an ankle-high barrier.

"Hard to believe this is cut every year from the ice and snow," Hattie said, her face going a shade paler as a rider whizzed by, the toboggan rattling over a bumpy patch of ice.

"Really? I had no idea."

"Oh, I've heard all about it. Rob is over the moon about being here and getting to ride the *hallowed* Cresta. He's a walking encyclopedia and rather toboggan-mad." Her voice took on the punchy tones of a film reel announcer. "It's nearly four thousand feet long and has a drop of nearly one hundred and sixty feet. They use a chronograph to time each rider and keep a record of the fastest times." She switched back to her normal speaking voice. "Would you like to know more?"

I laughed. "No, but your impression of a newsreader was spot-on. It's all very interesting. However, I don't have a head for figures, and I'll forget it all in a moment."

"Oh, they stick in my brain. Good thing, too, since I'm always cutting material and measuring off lengths of fabric and ribbon."

A cheer went up as a four-man toboggan whipped by so quickly it felt as if I would have missed it if I'd blinked. Hattie closed her eyes and swallowed, all the playfulness draining out of her demeanor. "I know it's all in good fun, and they can steer with their body weight by shifting their legs and feet—Rob's been reading up on it—but it does look brutal, what with them going headfirst."

I agreed but kept silent. She was already nervous for her husband, and I didn't want to amplify those feelings. "I'm sure they'll be fine." After all, toboggan after toboggan was flying by, gliding over the ice unscathed. Since she was gazing over my shoulder intensely now, looking up the run with her gloved hands clenched, I added, "I suppose it will be a while before they come down. There was quite a line."

She nodded. "I think this whole thing's rather absurd. Swishing down on a sled. It's basically a children's game that grown-ups play, but I'd never say that to Rob. He thinks it the height of manliness."

"Well, men must have their games, mustn't they?"

We shared a quick smile, then she said, "You must think Rob and I are quite callous to be out here the day after Emmaline's death, but it's not as if one can put on black and stay in one's room at the hotel for the rest of our time here." Her breath sent out little whiffs of white vapor in the raw air.

"I don't think anyone expects that of you."

She let out a sigh, creating more feathering plumes of white. "Emmaline and I were close—once—but that wasn't the case lately."

I looked down and stamped my feet, flattening the trail so I'd have a level place to stand as I spoke. "But you're partners in LaRue's."

She tilted her head in a gesture that indicated my statement was only a partial truth. The movement caused the froth of black curls that protruded from under the edge of her knit hat to bounce. "Emmaline put up the money, and I did all the work." She squinted up the run, her gaze focused on the next riders, then let out a gusty sigh. "And that was Emmaline in a nutshell. She wasn't one to get her hands dirty. She adored the idea of owning the shop, but she wasn't interested in the day-to-day running of it—budgets and inventory and restocking merchandise. No, that was far too plebeian for Emmaline. She'd sweep in and cause pots and pots of chaos with her grand plans and then drop out of sight for weeks or even months."

I kept my head down, toeing the snow with my boot as Hattie went silent for a moment, then she added, "We were only a few weeks into the venture when I realized it was a mistake—*such* a mistake. She had no idea about money, just spent and spent and spent. Penny-pincher that Ben is, I'm sure he was thrilled with the news about the renovations at Kulm because it meant they could stay at the Alpine House, which is much more economical. Emmaline would never holiday anywhere but in the very lap of luxury—unless there were renovations going on, of course. In that case, the Alpine House would do, but only in a pinch." She dug her hands into her coat pockets, pulling the fabric tight over her shoulders. "Now I see that it would've been better to have scrimped and saved for years and *then* opened the shop later on my own."

The cadence of her words had been speeding up, but she stopped abruptly. "I shouldn't speak ill of the dead. It is truly sad what happened to Emmaline, but I can honestly say that our friendship was a momentary thing, for a season. If we hadn't opened LaRue's together, we would probably have only spoken to each other occasionally, like at a party or the theater."

"Why is the millinery called LaRue's?" I asked to keep the conversation going.

"That's down to Emmaline. I have to give her credit there. She did have *some* good ideas. I wanted to call it Hattie's, but she insisted it wasn't a good choice. She said there would be nothing more absurd than Hattie's Hat Shop, and, of course, she was right. She suggested LaRue's because my middle name is Rue. LaRue's sounds French, and a whiff of anything related to France is always a benefit when it comes to fashion."

"That was astute."

"Emmaline did have a point about the name, but lately her ideas were so very absurd. She wanted to spend an enormous amount on newspaper ads and billboards. But the best advertisement we had was her wearing my hats and convincing her friends to visit the shop. She didn't seem to understand that. She was so set on doing things her way."

"Yes, I noticed that about her."

Her gaze switched from the track to my face. "I didn't realize you knew her."

"I only met her on the train, but it was clear that she had a . . . um . . . commanding manner. She knew exactly what she wanted and was adamant about it."

Hattie let out a little huff of a laugh. "That's putting it mildly." She dug her chin into her scarf, and the fringe of her curls hid her face as she looked down. "It's frightfully sad that she's died." She nudged a clump of snow with her boot. It fell off the trail and down to the track, landing with a little plop on the sleek curve of ice. "The whole situation is regrettable."

"You didn't happen to see her when you went to powder your nose last evening?"

"No. She'd gone straight up to bed. In fact, I didn't see anyone at all. The ladies' room was empty."

"Strange that Mrs. Lavington was on the terrace, though." I couldn't ask the sorts of questions Vogel could, but Mrs. Lavington's presence on the terrace late on a cold night was odd. It was the sort of observation that, while it might not be in the best of taste, wouldn't raise too many eyebrows. The situation was unusual, and people would comment on it.

"I stopped trying to figure out why Emmaline did anything a long time ago." She didn't sound as if she was curious at all about the death.

"It does sound as if working with her would be quite trying."

Hattie leaned to the side, her attention fixed on a point

farther up the run. "Oh, it was. Some days I wanted to ring her neck." She seemed to realize what she'd said, and her gaze snapped back to my face. "Not that I'd ever do anything to hurt her, not like that inspector bloke insinuated." One corner of her mouth quirked down. "Which is barmy! But I suppose being a lady detective, you're wondering about it too." She infused the words *lady detective* with doubt. "I mean, yes, I don't doubt Emmaline could have pushed someone to the point that they'd do her in, but everyone knows she was alone on the terrace with only her footprints in the snow."

"It sounds as if Korporale Vogel is just checking all possibilities," I said, my tone mild. I didn't want to get into the details of how Mrs. Lavington had been killed. I wanted to stay focused on the buyout negotiations. "Mrs. Lavington refusing to sell must have been incredibly frustrating."

Hattie snorted. "Emmaline would have taken the offer —eventually. I booked the hotel for a week because I knew it would take at least that long. She'd toy with me for a while, but in the end she'd sell. She'd take the money. Emmaline found it very hard to resist money. Besides, I was saving my best card to play later. I hadn't even told Rob about it. My trump card was that I'd arrange the sale and have the money put into a bank account that was solely hers. A play like that would have pleased her, to have a little nest egg all her own. I know she'd have taken that offer."

I stepped to the side so another spectator could squeeze by us. "Perhaps Rob took matters into his own hands."

When I looked up from shuffling back into place,

Hattie's furious glare hit me, and I instantly stepped back and tottered a moment on the snowy ledge. Her cheeks had gone from a tinge of pink in the cold air to a flood of deep red. She poked at the lapel of my coat. "Don't say things like that about Rob. Emmaline annoyed him to no end, but he'd never, *never* do anything to hurt her."

Arms out for balance, I said, "Steady there. I—"

Her glove shot out, nearly punching me in the face, as she pointed up the run. "Look, there's Rob! I recognize his coat." Her anger disappeared like a puff of smoke blown away in the wind. She clapped and yelled as the toboggan pelted by. I watched her out of the corner of my eye as I moved away from the edge. She wasn't paying any attention to me. Back turned to me, she was following the progress of the toboggan down the run.

A moment later Jasper came by in the next toboggan, his long form laid out at the front of the sled as it swept up into the curve. He flexed his shoulders as they came into the turn, which sent up a spray of ice crystals. They swished away almost before I had time to register the rising surge of worry that coursed through me. I suddenly understood Hattie's concern for Rob.

She gripped my arm. "Oh, thank goodness they'll be down in a few seconds. Let's go to the finish and meet them." She set off before I could respond.

I caught up with her, and we high-stepped down the snow to the end of the run, where we found the men in high spirits. There was much back-slapping and hand-shaking interspersed with detailed analysis of the runs.

Eventually, Jasper glanced at the mountains. One side of the valley was already coated in shadow. The layer of darkness was creeping across the lake, dousing the sparkling reflection of the bright sky. "Don't think we'll have time for another run."

"Good," Hattie said firmly and looped her arm through Rob's. I eyed her, wondering if she was still riled up, but she didn't charge toward me, which I took to be a good sign. Her high color had faded back to the usual rosiness brought on by the alpine air, and her tone was cheery as she said, "We still have to trek back to the hotel. By the time we get there, it will be time to dress for dinner. We'll see you all there."

I didn't get an opportunity to speak to Jasper on the way back to the hotel. Mr. Hale was fairly buzzing with energy and stayed with us all the way back, talking about ways to fine-tune their runs to shave seconds off their time. We went our separate ways to change for dinner. I was certainly ready for dinner since I'd missed lunch and only had tea and cakes that afternoon. After the hike up to the toboggan run and back, I was famished. I intended to enjoy the hearty meal. No dainty portions for me.

I was seated at a table with Hattie and Rob, along with Jasper and two newly arrived guests. Mr. Blinkhorn rounded out our party. Hattie had been polite and had even smiled at me when we were seated, but I was glad I wasn't near her. I didn't want to encounter her white-hot temper during dinner. Across the table from me, Jasper was deep in conversation with a silver-haired dowager, discussing a recent play. Mr. Blinkhorn was on my left. Thanks to Vogel's sharp observation of the dimple, I'd been able to greet my dinner companion by name instead of mumbling something unintelligible that might pass for an acknowledgment. He informed me that Mr. Lavington had arranged for another mountaineer to take over their climbing lessons the next day. He buttered a roll as he said, "Not sure I'm as keen on climbing as I was. I'd like to give the Cresta another go."

"I could tell it was quite a thrilling experience for you all."

"Have you ever thought of giving it a try yourself?"

I shook my head. "I'm to have a skiing lesson tomorrow, so I'll stick with that for now. Perhaps you could put off your climbing lesson for a day or two and tackle the Cresta again."

"No, couldn't do that. Wouldn't be sporting, after Mr. Lavington went out of his way to set it up, even after all that's happened," Mr. Blinkhorn said. "Old Smithers will do fine, I'm sure. But he doesn't have the . . . zest Mr. Lavington has."

"So Mr. Lavington is a good climber, then?"

Mr. Blinkhorn swallowed his bite as he nodded. "He's the best climber alive today—excellent technique, but not plodding or pedestrian. Stylish. And he knows when to take a bit of a risk." He let out a long breath and reached for his wine. "It is disappointing we won't be able to climb with him."

The next course arrived, and I turned to speak to Rob. "Did you enjoy the Cresta Run?"

He picked up his wineglass that the waiter had just refilled. "Yes, indeed. Can't wait to do it again." He set the glass down very carefully. The ruddiness of his complexion was heightened. It might have been due to the alpine sun, but I suspected it had more to do with the many glasses of the excellent wine he'd consumed. "Today the run was a little spongy from the sun." He spoke the sentence slowly, carefully enunciating the words. "After this evening, when there's a good hard freeze, we'll go in the morning. It will be even faster then."

"Do you ski as well?"

"No. I have no interest in sk-sk-," he amended, "going about with planks on my feet."

We talked of winter sports for a few moments, and then he said abruptly, "How were you acquainted with Emmaline?"

Surprised at the abrupt change of tack, I kept my answer short. "I met her on the train."

He rested his wrist on the edge of the table as he turned to me fully and fixed his rather bleary gaze on me. "But I saw her go into your compartment. She was in there for quite a long time."

"Just a little girl talk."

He gave me a disbelieving look and went back to cutting his meat. "I only ask because I have to watch out for Hattie. She's too soft-hearted. Gets taken in." He paused, a morsel of meat on the tines of his fork. "So you were a friend of Emmaline's, and she wanted you to convince Hattie not to buy her out, and . . ." He seemed to lose his train of thought and frowned at his plate, then he sat more upright. "Doesn't matter what you say." He waved his fork at me. "Hattie's buying her out."

Clearly, he was more muddled than I realized since he seemed to have forgotten that Emmaline wasn't around to be bought out. "I don't plan to give your wife business advice. She seems quite savvy in that area."

"Not when it comes to Emmaline. Hattie tries to stand

up to her, but Emmaline plows right over anyone in her path. She'll run the shop into the ground. No head for business, that one. But she insith—" He swallowed. "Emmaline wants Hattie to fall in line with her barmy ideas. Hattie would be better off without her around."

Across the table, Hattie was sending her husband a glare. The intensity of it could have rivaled the sun, but Rob was oblivious.

Rob's voice was loud and carried across the table to his wife, but I spoke more softly so that no one else could hear me except Rob. "Last evening when you left the lounge to get the drinks, did you happen to see Emmaline?"

He picked up his wine again and shook his head. "No, I went straight to the other bar and came back. Didn't see her at all."

"Do you know why Mrs. Lavington went to the terrace?" I wanted to get his opinion—wine-soaked as it was—on the topic.

He tossed back a gulp of wine, then lifted his shoulders and turned his mouth down in a *who knows* look. "Emmaline's daft. She's always doing bonkers things. Like that treasure hunt. She sh—" He slowed his words. "She should have known better than to race around in motors on an icy night," he said, pronouncing each word with care.

"I don't think I heard about that."

"Sad business, that. I don't blame Mrs. Ath—" He paused, swallowed, and tried again. "Mrs. *Ash*ford at all for being steamed up. Sad business."

And even though I asked him about it again, he simply repeated the same phrase. I changed tacks. Since the fact that Mrs. Lavington had died seemed to have completely gone out of his head, I didn't even try to bring up any of my suspicions related to her death. Instead, I phrased my next question in the present tense, hoping that matching up with his thoughts would get an answer. "What do you think Hattie will do if Emmaline won't sell to her?"

"Hattie will convince her. Somehow." He gave a slow nod to emphasize his point. "Once Hattie gets something in her mind . . ." He pointed his fork at his head as he said this, and for a moment I thought he might put his eye out, but he lowered his hand. "She goes at it full force."

"But what if Hattie can't get Mrs. Lavington to change her mind? Hattie has a bit of temper . . ."

Rob chuckled. "That she does. Like a little terrier, is Hattie. Yap up a storm and then forget all in the next minute."

"So you don't think she'd harm Mrs. Lavington?"

"Hattie?" He pulled his chin in and tried to focus on my face. "Nah. She's smarter than that."

"What about you?"

"Eh?" He leaned in, the muscles around his eyes flexing as he squinted.

"Would *you* hurt Mrs. Lavington?" It was an impertinent question, but I doubted he'd remember this conversation.

Candlelight flashed as he swished the knife, mirroring the swivel of his head back and forth. "I would never thrike—strike—a lady. Bad form. Not cricket."

As pudding was served, I turned with some relief to Mr. Blinkhorn to hear more about the particulars of tobogganing. After several minutes of discourse, I managed to divert us from the topic of winter sport. "I understand you and Mr. Hale are related?" I looked across the room to where Mr. Hale sat, focused on his food, and not contributing much to the conversation.

"Indeed, Miss Belgrave. Everyone supposes we're brothers, if not twins, but we're cousins. Our mothers were twins, though, so there is that. Funnily enough, they don't look much alike. Fraternal twins. They almost married two brothers who were twins, but that didn't happen. It's a cracking good story . . ."

By the end of dinner, I was able to add another point of difference between the two men. Mr. Blinkhorn was *much* chattier than his cousin.

CHAPTER 18

*L*ater that evening Jasper and I were settled on a sofa in the lounge, holding hands as we watched the dying fire in the grate. The room looked entirely normal. Some chairs had been rearranged to fill the gap where the burnt chair had been removed. A new hearthrug lay in front of the fire, but otherwise there was no indication that a guest's clothing had caught fire in the room.

Jasper and I had played chess until most of the other hotel guests had turned in. A group of strangers remained in the back of the room by the bar, playing cards, but they'd taken no interest in us, so we essentially had the other half of the room to ourselves. While enjoying the warmth of the fire and the sensation of Jasper's thumb running across the back of my hand, I'd caught him up on everything that had happened that day.

He lifted his gin and tonic with his free hand. "So you've been brought into the official investigation. Congratulations, old bean."

"Thank you, but it remains to be seen if I'm able to contribute to discovering what really happened to Mrs. Lavington."

"I'm sure you'll suss something out. You always do."

"I did learn a few things today." I recounted my conversations with Hattie and Rob. "Hattie has a mercurial temper, but I'm not sure if either one of them would have actually resorted to violence. Even though he was three sheets to the wind, Rob was still quite adamant that he'd never hurt a lady."

"Quite so. It's the only proper way to behave." Jasper contemplated the embers. "I've never heard anything unsavory about Rob Grogan. I don't know anything about Hattie and Rob or their relationship with Emmaline either, but I can shed some light on Rob's comments about Mrs. Ashford."

"Do tell."

"I'm afraid it's a sad story."

"Those were the exact words that Rob used."

Releasing my hand, Jasper turned and placed his arm along the back of the sofa. He surveyed the room. Apparently content that no one would overhear him, he turned back to me. "Emmaline hosted a party. It had been one of those freakishly beautiful days that we sometimes get in London in early spring. Felt as if summer was right around the corner, but late that afternoon the weather changed. A storm moved in. Foul night. Sleety rain and wind blowing it right in your face. This was several years ago, not long after the war ended. 'Twenty or 'twenty-one, I think. Emmaline had planned a scavenger hunt around London for after-dinner entertainment."

Jasper took a long sip of his drink before continuing.

"The rain cleared, but it was frigid. I remember because I returned from an engagement that evening and slipped on the pavement. Nearly took a header down a set of basement steps, but I managed to catch the iron railings. Once I was safely home, I tucked myself in front of the fire with a good book and stayed put. I heard about Emmaline's party the next day at my club. Friend of mine, Lawrence Gilquist, had been there."

I shifted on the sofa so that I was facing him. His voice was so subdued, and his words were hesitant. It was almost as if he didn't want to tell the story. A fluttery feeling of dread stirred in me.

Jasper went on. "Gilquist said some of the guests wanted to cancel the treasure hunt, but Emmaline insisted, saying the rain had stopped and it would be great fun. Gilquist said they slipped and slid across London gathering up clues to win the game. They were on Pall Mall when one of the motors skidded on the ice toward another one, an open two-seater. The driver jerked the steering wheel to avoid a smash. Mrs. Ashford's son, Howard, was the passenger. He was standing up, yelling instructions to a friend in another motor. He was thrown and injured."

"Oh, that's terrible." I had a horrible, sinking feeling about how the story ended.

"It was. He was injured quite badly. Several broken bones, but apparently it was the injury to his head that was the worst of the lot. He lingered a few days, then passed."

"Poor Mrs. Ashford. And she's a widow, isn't she?" I seemed to recall the article I'd read about her mentioned she and her husband had met while climbing. After he died, she'd carried on mountaineering with other lady climbers.

"I don't know the details of her husband's death, but I believe she'd been a widow many years when the incident happened. Gilquist was in our club the day after and was badly shaken. As one would be. He said Mrs. Ashford was climbing in the French Alps and had been summoned home." Jasper sipped his drink. "She returned in time to see Howard before he died." Jasper tilted his glass, watching the liquid slosh to the side. "He was her only child."

"Life is just beastly at times," I said in a small voice.

"Quite so," Jasper agreed. We didn't need to say anything else. I leaned into his shoulder a bit more.

He added, "It was the talk of London for a while. Mrs. Ashford bore it somehow, stiff upper lip and all that. The accident was investigated, of course, and the decision was that, while the roads were icy, it wasn't the driver's fault. Howard had been standing up in the motor."

"It must have been dreadful for Mrs. Ashford." A log shifted, falling into the embers, and the fire popped. I said, "How would you move on from something like that?"

Jasper lifted his arm in a shrug. "I don't know. Just keep plugging along, I suppose, as one does. Gilquist was cut up about the whole thing. Used me as a sounding board. He'd been a close friend of Howard's, and Mrs. Ashford had asked his opinion on whether or not she could bring legal proceedings against Emmaline, but in the end, Mrs. Ashford dropped the idea."

"Because Emmaline organized the scavenger hunt?"

"No, because she was driving the motor Howard was in." Jasper leaned forward to place his empty glass on the table. "It's been years since it happened. At least three, maybe longer."

"Even so, I understand why Mrs. Ashford looked so disapproving on the train when she saw Emmaline's group."

"I could have told you about the history between Emmaline and Mrs. Ashford, but I—"

"Didn't want to gossip, which is good of you. But I'm glad you told me now. I suppose I'll have to pass the information to Vogel."

I settled back against the cushion and looped my arm around his so we could hold hands again. "Although in the dining car Mrs. Ashford looked disapproving, not murderous."

Jasper rubbed his free hand along the seam in the sofa arm absently. "However, she was one of the people who left the lounge last night. Opportunity and motive."

"True. But then we bump up against the means. If Mrs. Ashford arranged, shall we say, Mrs. Lavington's accident, how did she do it? I can't work out those details—for her or anyone else. And that's to say nothing of finding proof."

"It's a sticky wicket, I agree."

I studied the crisscross pattern of glowing veins in the embers of the charred wood as Jasper said, "It's such an extreme thing to kill someone. Would someone really do it to be rid of a business partner or for revenge, years later?"

"It's not what one does in the normal course of things, but there's that whispered conversation I overheard. Two people obviously thought they were coming up to a time that was the perfect opportunity to get rid of someone. One of them definitely mentioned the difficulty of getting rid of a body with the frozen ground, and the other person's reply was along the lines of it was *worked out*. A death that appears to be an accident would be written off."

"No hiding of a body needed in that scenario," Jasper said.

"And there are quite a few pairs in the group of people who knew Mrs. Lavington." I ticked them off on my fingers. "Rob and Hattie. Mrs. Ashford and Juliet. They were both on the train and work together. And then there's Etta and her doorman, Fredrick."

"He wasn't on the train, though. You said he was working here at the hotel when we arrived."

"Yes, good point."

"And the two young climbers, Hale and Blinkhorn, are friends," Jasper said. "Possibly relatives?"

"Yes, cousins, but there's nothing covert about those two." I told him about how Vogel had confirmed the two men were away from the hotel last evening. "They're here to climb and toboggan, as I found out in extreme detail at dinner. Nothing furtive about them."

"Unlike the lady's maid and the doorman."

"Exactly. There's something going on there, but I'm not sure what. I wish I could find out more about them. They obviously knew each other, and, from their shocked expressions on the day we arrived, it was clear they were both surprised to see the other."

I didn't tell Jasper, but I planned to engineer a meeting with Etta tomorrow. "Perhaps Vogel will discover something."

"Ah, Vogel again."

I shifted to look at Jasper's face, but he stood and

picked up the poker. "Why the tone? You sound ... nettled."

"No. Nothing like that. Vogel's a fine chap, I'm sure. Don't mind me. Fire's about out," Jasper said. "Should I stir it up?"

"No, I'm ready to turn in. Are you going back to your —er—project?"

"Yes, probably for a few hours. I find some of my most absurd ideas come to me after midnight."

"And absurd ideas are needed to solve your puzzle?"

"Sometimes it's the absurd idea that makes everything fall into place. Sort of a left turn and end-run around logic that gets the old brain cells tap-dancing in a new direction. Now there's a mixed metaphor for you." He stood and extended a hand to help me up. "What are you plans for tomorrow? Bebe said something about sleigh rides as one of the must-do activities. Are you interested?"

"Sounds lovely. I'm to have a ski lesson with Juliet in the afternoon, but my evening is open."

We rode the lift up together, which we had to ourselves. We took full advantage of the privacy to share a good-night kiss.

CHAPTER 19

The next morning, after breakfast, I went back up to my room and took out one of the heavy velvet dresses that I'd brought to wear while ice-skating. I worked a pencil into the side seam and gave it a good yank, cringing as it ripped. It was a beautiful frock that my cousin Gwen had handed off to me, and I hated to damage it, but it was for a good cause. My skills as a seamstress were not exceedingly high, but I'd be able to repair it if worse came to worst. Hopefully, I wouldn't need to.

I went down the hall and knocked on the door at the far end. Etta opened the door a sliver. It only took her a few seconds to wipe the surprised look off her face and replace it with polite interest. "Miss Belgrave, good morning."

"Good morning, Etta. I was wondering if you might help me? I have a tear in one of my dresses that I intended to wear while skating. Would you be able to mend it? I'd appreciate any help you could give me, and I'll be happy to pay you for your time and effort."

She glanced at the dress. "Of course, Miss Belgrave. But you don't have to pay me. It won't take but a moment. Would you like to step inside and wait while I do it?" She swung the door wide. "Or, if you'd rather, I can bring it to you later."

"I don't mind waiting." In fact, it was just what I'd hoped she'd say. She left the door open and moved a stack of folded clothes from the single chair in the room, transferring them to the bed, where a partially packed suitcase was splayed open.

I perched on the chair beside a small table with several magazines on it. "Packing to leave?"

Etta took a small wooden box from the bureau. Her soft peach skirt, which matched her jumper, twirled around her legs as she turned, scooted the suitcase over, and took a seat on the bed. "Yes, I finished repacking Mrs. Lavington's things. Mr. Lavington says the household no longer needs me."

It wasn't unexpected, but it did seem rather abrupt. "I hope you find work in England quickly."

She folded back the lid of the box and plucked out two small spools of thread, then held them against the dress, her face softening as she said, "Oh, I'm not going back to England. Only to Promontogno."

"Really? I'm not familiar with it."

"It's a beautiful village with an old stone mill and views of a glacier." She returned one of the spools to the box, then removed a pair of scissors, a thimble, and a card of needles.

"You've visited it before?"

"No, I've only been told about it, but I'll see it tomorrow." She kept her head bent as she threaded the needle. A smile had flooded her face.

"What's happened?" I asked. I could hear the happiness in her words.

She looked up immediately, her hands dropping to her lap. "I'm going to live with Fredrick's family until the wedding."

"Wedding?" For the first time, I noticed the thin gold band on her finger. "You're engaged. To Fredrick? He's the doorman here, isn't he?"

She nodded, a blush suffusing her cheeks as she turned the frock inside out and arranged the velvet so that the ripped seam lined up. She pinned it in place with quick, efficient moves. She didn't look worried or scared, as she had the last time we spoke. With her pink cheeks, creamy skin, and her hair in a becoming chignon, she looked elegant and attractive. With the less severe hairstyle and softer colors, she no longer looked like a lady's maid.

"My goodness! Well, congratulations. Best wishes to you both."

"Thank you." She looked up quickly, flashed a blinding smile, then returned her attention to the fabric. "It's grand. I'm still gobsmacked at seeing Fredrick again. After what happened—I never thought—it seemed utterly impossible—" She sniffed, overcome by emotion, then swallowed and regained her composure. "Pardon me, Miss Belgrave. It's just that I'm so very, very happy, and I didn't expect it. I'm bowled over by it, I am." The silver of the needle flashed in and out of the velvet.

"Now I'm curious. You must tell me what happened."

The stitches slowed, and she angled her head to the

side. "When I think of the chances of it—of the Lavingtons arranging to stay in the exact hotel where Fredrick worked . . ." She gave me another bemused smile. Then she said in a quiet, more somber voice, "It's tragic what happened to Mrs. Lavington, it truly is. I wish it hadn't happened to her, but being here and seeing Fredrick again . . ." She shrugged, as if to say she couldn't put her emotion into words, and went back to sewing.

"You knew Fredrick in England, then?"

"Oh yes. For years. He worked for Mrs. Lavington's father. He was Mr. Grayson's valet."

"I didn't realize."

She continued with the rapid, tiny stitches. "I don't imagine many people know."

"And you worked for Mrs. Lavington then, before she married?"

"Yes, she was Miss Grayson at that point. I went into service with the Grayson family when I was twelve. I've been her lady's maid since she came out."

"And you and Fredrick developed . . . an understanding?"

She nodded, a shadow falling across her face. "Mr. Grayson, he didn't forbid the servants to step out with one another, but Miss Emmaline—well, she had a different opinion. Mr. Grayson was poorly, and Fredrick said it was best to keep our understanding a secret, what with Mr. Grayson being so ill. Mrs. Grayson had passed a few years before, so Miss Emmaline was mistress of the house. Mr. Grayson wouldn't oppose us, but with Miss Emmaline . . . it was different. She always said it wasn't good for the servants to step out. Led to slackness and daydreaming, she said. Hardly anyone on the staff knew about me and Fredrick, except the housekeeper, but she turned a blind eye. Mrs. Heavers didn't particularly like Miss Emmaline, you see. Fredrick and I were very discreet."

"I can imagine."

Etta stopped sewing and looked across the room, her gaze unfocused. "But then Mr. Grayson died, and Miss Emmaline called Fredrick into the little morning room where she did the accounts. She accused him of *carrying on*, as she called it, with someone on the staff. She told him that unless he told her who it was, she'd let him go without a reference. Fredrick, being the gentleman that he is, refused to tell her anything."

Etta went back to stitching. "She had him pack his bag and leave. I was in London, picking up an evening gown for Miss Emmaline, and he was gone when I returned. Fredrick couldn't find work in England. Without a reference, it was difficult, but his uncle owns a guesthouse in Promontogno. He arranged for Fredrick to take a job here at the Alpine House because they didn't need anyone in Promontogno at that time. But now his uncle is getting on in years. He's selling the guesthouse to Fredrick. We are going to run it."

"How wonderful that the story has a happy ending. But didn't you keep in touch? Didn't you know where Fredrick was?" I found it hard to believe they hadn't communicated, but there was that shocked look on both of their faces when Etta arrived at Alpine House. I didn't think they could have manufactured that.

"No, we couldn't." A trace of her earlier anxiety shadowed Etta's face. "Miss Emmaline checked all the post when it came in, every single piece. She believed that if you worked in her household, she had a right to see every bit of correspondence. If I'd received a letter from Switzerland, she'd have demanded to know what it was about."

"How intrusive."

Etta didn't reply, but I sensed agreement in her silence. I imagined she'd had to guard her words for years. Habits like that didn't disappear quickly. She stretched the fabric and studied the seam. "Fredrick had managed to leave me a note—the housekeeper handed it off without telling Miss Emmaline—and he said he'd send for me when he was able. But then Miss Emmaline married. I went with her when she moved. I was glad to have the job. My parents had both died during the Spanish flu, so I had nowhere else to go. Mrs. Heavers said she'd forward any post to a private box I had in London, but then she fell ill, and I didn't know how to reach Fredrick. It was all quite frustrating and dismal, but then when I saw him when we arrived, it was like . . ." She heaved a joyful sigh as she tried to describe her emotions. "It was like the sun breaking through the clouds after a storm."

"I imagine your Fredrick was quite upset with Mrs. Lavington, though."

"Yes. He was vexed. I could see it on his face. But once we met and were able to talk, we sorted everything out."

"It's all happened so quickly."

"Yes, but we don't want to waste any more time. It's like a fairy tale, isn't it? I'll live in a beautiful mountain village with Fredrick. I'll be mistress of the guesthouse." She tested the strength of the knot at the end of her line of stitches and then snipped off the thread. "It's incredibly sad what happened to Mrs. Lavington, though." She turned the dress inside out and examined the stitches from the other side.

"What do you think Mr. Lavington will do?" I asked.

"I suppose eventually he'll find some nice young lady who enjoys sport, unlike Mrs. Lavington."

"I understand she was delicate."

The muscles around Etta's mouth flattened, giving her a look that showed she disagreed with my statement.

"Mrs. Lavington *said* she was delicate. She had glandular fever when she was a child and was mollycoddled all her life. She insisted that she never be exposed to cold or drafts and never do anything that required any physical exertion." Etta leaned toward me and lowered her voice a notch. "She enjoyed the attention of being fragile. She was lovely to look at—a real beauty. Mr. Lavington fell in love with that face and figure of hers, but I imagine he'll be much happier if he finds somebody who enjoys tramping in the mountains. There are plenty of women here who are of his class who enjoy skating and skiing, and there's even some lady climbers." She shook out the dress, folded it expertly with a few quick flicks of her wrist, and handed it to me.

"Has Mr. Lavington shown any interest in anyone in particular?"

"No, they were both quite loyal," she said as we moved to the door. "Bit surprising, seeing as how they were so different personality-wise. Of course, Mr. Lavington was away quite a lot. I don't know what he got up to during those times."

"And how is he now?"

"Right broken up. He hasn't left their suite. The hotel keeps sending up trays, but he only picks at the food, then sends it back. He doesn't want the drapes open, and if I hadn't stoked the fire, it would have been arctic cold in there." She pressed her lips together and made a tsking sound. "He just sits there in the dark, smoking. I was glad to finish packing Mrs. Lavington's things and leave him be." She swung the door open.

"Are you sure I can't pay you for this?"

"There's no need. Just being able to share my happiness with someone has been wonderful. Consider it a thank-you for having a word with that police inspector fellow for me. He only asked me two questions. He was most interested in how I spent my time on the night Mrs. Lavington—er—passed, and he hasn't bothered me at all since then."

"I see. Well, that's good to hear. Out of curiosity, what were you doing that evening?"

She motioned to the straight-back chair. "I was here, reading, while I waited for Mrs. Lavington to summon me to help her change after dinner. She never called for me."

As I stepped into the hall, I asked, "And what was the other question Korporale Vogel asked?"

"My shoe size! I thought it was daft, I really did. But he'd said it was his last question, and if I'd answer it, he'd be on his way. He kept his word—well, he did have a look at my shoe as well, but he hasn't bothered me again. Thank you again for smoothing the way for me with the police." She dropped her voice on the last word, even though the corridor was empty.

"I'm glad it hasn't been difficult for you. Although you should definitely let Korporale Vogel know about your engagement and where you'll be."

She rubbed her thumb across a thin, gold band on her finger. "Perhaps I'll have Fredrick do it."

I agreed that would be a good idea and went back to my room to change into the velvet dress so I could take a few turns on the ice—after I visited Korporal Vogel. I had quite a bit to tell him.

CHAPTER 20

*I*t was another brilliantly sunny day, but a layer of gray clouds swathed the tips of the mountains on the far side of the lake. Perhaps another snowfall was on the way, but for now, people were out, eyes narrowed against the glare of the sparkling snow. I lifted my face to the dazzling sunlight as I walked along the lanes. Even with a deep blanket of snow and the cold air, it was pleasant outdoors. If I'd been doing some sort of exercise like skating or snowshoeing, I wouldn't have even needed my coat on to keep warm. It was such a contrast to a typical gray damp February day in London.

"Olive!" I turned to see Jasper hurrying down the steps of the hotel. "Care for a walk?"

"Yes, that would be lovely. I'm going to see Vogel, but I can put that off for a quarter hour. How's your—um—work coming along?"

Jasper tucked his scarf under his coat lapels. "It's taking much longer than I thought. I'm sorry about that, old bean. I need a short ramble. A bit of fresh air to keep me sharp."

"Perhaps a walk in the woods?" I asked as we reached the corner of the hotel. Jasper agreed, and we turned left and walked along the lane that climbed up the mountain. The air was fragrant with the scent of pine. Rhythmic drips of melting snow plopped into snowy puddles, a counterpoint to the rush of wind in the treetops.

"Seeing the korporale again?" Jasper's tone was tight, so unlike his usual jaunty conversation, but he smiled at me and extended his arm as we came to an area with an icy patch.

I took his arm. "Yes, a few details have come to light that he should know about. Take all the time you need with your project. I'm quite happy to spend my time alternating between alpine activities and poking about, trying to figure out what really happened to Mrs. Lavington."

"Yes, you do enjoy your puzzles." His inflection was odd. I looked up at him as we passed the rooftop restaurant and the grade of the road steepened. "Jasper, are you perturbed?"

"Me? Perturbed?"

"Yes. You don't sound like yourself."

He cleared his throat. "Too much time shut up in the hotel room, I expect. I am a bit exasperated—about my project. Yes, that's it. I'm irked that it's taking longer than I expected. Now tell me about your puzzle. Any progress?"

"A bit. Oh, look, there's Mr. Lavington." He was inching along the side of the road, his back to us. With his hands in his pockets, his shoulders rounded forward, and his chest sunk inward, his silhouette had a hollowed-out aspect to it. "I haven't been able to talk to him at all because he's kept to his room."

Jasper called out, "Lavington!"

Mr. Lavington started and spun around, sliding on a patch of ice. His hands shot out of his pockets for balance, and he did some fancy footwork to stay upright. During his jerky movements, his hat fell off and tumbled down the slope to us.

Jasper snatched it up before it could roll all the way down the lane. "Sorry, old chap." Jasper dusted snow from the fedora's brim and handed it back. "Didn't mean to give you a fright."

"Not at all. Lost in my thoughts." Mr. Lavington's appearance was quite a contrast to the urbane moun- taineer I'd seen on the train. He hadn't shaved, and the dark growth of his beard blurred his jawline. He jammed the hat on his greasy hair. Above us, a burst of laughter floated down from the sun terrace. "I'm out for a bit of a ramble," he added, his tone muted. His gaze ranged over the trees and up the stone retaining wall. "My room was too stuffy."

"Yes, I'm familiar with that," Jasper said. "Do join us. We're going up to the top of the hill."

"All right," Mr. Lavington agreed in a dull tone and fell into step with us. For a while, the only sound was the crunch of our steps on the snow and our labored breathing that created white clouds as we puffed up the incline. We reached a plateau where the road leveled out and then ran into a dense forest. Fallen pine needles, brown and spongy, softened our steps. I was running through options for small talk, but everything from *Gorgeous view* to *Beautiful weather we're having* sounded trite or inappropriate for a conversation with a man whose wife had just died.

Mr. Lavington paused and put his hand on a thick wooden signpost that pointed up another track. He patted it and looked around, his attention sharpening like a sleepwalker coming back to reality. "I came this way the night Emmaline died."

"Would you like to turn back?" I asked.

"No. Let's go on. I don't want to go back to that stifling box of a room yet. I apologize, to be so badly behaved and tromp along in silence."

"Chitchat is highly overrated, especially in a place like this," Jasper said, indicating the snowy forest with its evergreen boughs layered with snow and the patch of startling blue sky visible through the treetops.

"I quite agree." He gave us a brief, tired smile, then rubbed his hand across the letters burned into the wooden signpost. "I had to use my lighter to see the direction. It was black as pitch when I came along here." He walked on and pointed to a chalet tucked back from the lane. "That house had a light on. I could see the number, a one, carved into the lentil. So I went along . . ." He narrated as we strode along the lane, his voice becoming strong and his pace increasing. "I could see lights at number three, there, and farther ahead at number five."

The chalets were spaced widely apart, each on about half an acre of land. When we came to the next house, he paused and scrubbed his hand over his stubble. "Number seven was dark." The chalet he nodded to was set closer to the lane. A little sign nailed to a tree trunk read *For Let* in German and English, but even without the notice it would have been obvious the chalet wasn't occupied. The shutters on the two windows on the upper story were closed, giving it the look of a sleeping face. A snow drift several inches deep covered the threshold and half of the front door. "I stood here a moment or two, trying to work out what to do. I realized I must have got the address wrong, so instead of rousing the neighbors, I ran back to the hotel. My German's mostly limited to climbing terms, so I would have been rubbish at asking where to go for help. When I'd run out of the lounge, I'd asked one of the hotel staff for the nearest doctor's address. I'd heard *seven*, but I found out later that the correct address was *seventeen*. I was too hasty and ran off without confirming the house number." He turned away and patted his pockets. "I need a cigarette."

"Here you are," Jasper said and took out his case.

Once Mr. Lavington had lit up, he stared at the desolate chalet, blowing smoke out of the corner of his mouth, away from our group. I said, "You must have been discombobulated. It's a shame there was no one else out walking along the lane who you could ask. Mrs. Ashford and Juliet are staying at one of the chalets. It must be along here somewhere."

"I don't know where those chalets are. Probably somewhere nearer the hotel, I'd imagine." He turned and headed back to the signpost at the head of the lane.

He'd picked up his pace, and I tugged Jasper along. He was more of an ambler than a sprinter. "Did you see Mrs. Ashford?" I asked when we came level with him.

"No. But someone else could have been out here. It was dark as a cave. I didn't see another soul. Or hear anyone, for that matter. Snow deadens sound—muffles it."

We retraced our steps with Mr. Lavington leading the way.

He moved with a quick, sure-footed stride, deftly avoiding the shiny patches of ice. I followed in his footsteps and was nearly trotting by the time we neared the town. Going down was easier than going up, but I drew a deep, restorative breath of the clear alpine air when we turned the corner at the hotel.

Mr. Lavington threw his smoldering cigarette butt into the snow. "Thanks for the company." He wasn't even winded. His lips lifted along with his fingers, as if he wasn't quite sure how to smile but was giving it his best effort. He turned and pulled the brim of his hat lower over his eyes before he jogged up the steps of the hotel.

"He put on a burst of speed going down, didn't he?" I said between gulps of icy air. "Do you think he didn't like my questions?"

"Hard to tell. Perhaps withdrawn and being short with people is his normal manner," Jasper said as we watched him duck around some people leaving the hotel.

"He didn't seem that way on the train at breakfast. But he was rather chatty about the chalets just now. He was quite clear about his movements. It was only when I asked if he'd seen anyone that he cut me off and sprinted down like a mountain goat."

"Well, he is a climber. Perhaps that's his normal pace on easy descents," Jasper said.

CHAPTER 21

I left Jasper to his deciphering and set off toward the police station. I passed the town's sledding run, where children and adults alike were gliding —or sometimes falling—down the gradual slope, the air filled with excited shouts and laughter. I climbed the steps to the police station and stamped the snow from my boots. I reached for the door, but before I could grasp the handle, it opened.

"Allow me." Fredrick, Etta's fiancé, held it for me.

"Thank you, Mr. Klein."

"I have plenty of experience in this area," he added with a hint of a smile. The rage and tension that I'd seen on his face when he'd first spotted Mrs. Lavington was gone. His expression was open and bright. Considering that he was leaving the police station, his relaxed manner seemed to indicate he had nothing weighing on his mind. Perhaps it was just that he was in love and that made his outlook rosier. Or was he good at hiding his true feelings?

As I went through the door, he touched the brim of his hat. "Good day, Miss Belgrave."

If the word wasn't out already, the news that I was talking with the police would circulate through the hotel now. The door closed behind Fredrick Klein, and I turned to the young man who'd taken notes during the first round of Vogel's interviews. "Hello, Mr. Oberwaller." I opted for that title because I wasn't sure of his rank. "I'd like to speak to Korporale Vogel, if he's available."

I seemed to have stunned him speechless. Perhaps not many women stopped by the police station to chat with the korporale. Vogel appeared in the doorway of the office down the hall. He lifted the small cup of coffee he held. "Miss Belgrave. Come back, and we'll have a snug chat, if that is the expression?" The music filtering out of the radio today was Bach, heavier and darker than the light, airy Chopin had been.

"Perhaps you mean *cozy* chat," I said as he closed the door and came around his desk, but then I caught the twinkle in his eye. "Now you're teasing me—or pulling my leg, perhaps?"

"Oh yes, another excellent English idiom. So expressive." He turned off the radio. "Coffee?"

"Thank you, but no." I sat down in front of his desk. "I met Fredrick Klein on my way in. I talked with Etta this morning and heard what happened between her and Fredrick, how Mrs. Lavington let him go and they were separated."

"Yes, I asked him to come in and clear up a few details," Vogel said. "He was very forthcoming about his background and his connection with Miss Morgan. Apparently, it's a love story between those two."

"Amazing that they should run across each other again here in St. Moritz."

Vogel sipped his coffee. "We do have the distinction of being one of the foremost destinations of the wealthy—a winter playground, we're called sometimes. Mr. and Mrs. Lavington certainly fit into the class of tourists who visit here. It's not unusual that they would travel here and that Mrs. Lavington would bring her maid with her."

"But to stay at the same hotel as Etta's long-lost love?"

"I'm sure Miss Etta Morgan had no hand in the reservations. A lady's maid rarely has input of that nature. Mr. Lavington said Alpine House was his choice. Mrs. Lavington wanted to stay at Kulm, but then they learned of the renovations, and he selected Alpine House instead. Let us compare notes about the stories of Mr. Klein, doorman, and Miss Morgan, lady's maid." He settled back in his chair as I recounted what Etta had told me.

When I finished, Vogel put his small cup into the saucer on his desk. "That agrees with Mr. Klein's account."

"And although he seems quite chipper today, he certainly had a motive."

"Yes, that is true, but he was on duty in the lobby the entire time in question. There's no doubt about that. I confirmed it with hotel employees, as well as guests coming and going throughout the evening. And I can't quite picture Miss Etta Morgan killing her employer and setting up an elaborate scheme to make it look as if it were an accident. Miss Morgan says she spent the evening alone in her room reading."

A hint of suspicion tinged his words, so I said, "That does happen occasionally, a quiet evening with a book."

He blew out a breath. "It does, and with her mousy

attitude she seems an unlikely candidate to do in her employer. However, it would be so much nicer for me if she'd spent her time with some of the hotel staff while waiting for Mrs. Lavington to call for her."

He lifted his chin and focused on something behind me. I twisted around. A large blackboard on wheels filled the wall behind the door. Names ran down the left-hand side and across the top. The location of each person was noted throughout the evening. Some jotted phrases— questions or notes, perhaps—were listed on the right-hand side and, under those, several photos had been taped up. They were of the terrace before Mrs. Lavington's body had been removed.

"Goodness! I've never seen anything like this." The stark images were arresting, especially one that must have been taken from a balcony above. It showed in sharply delineated black and white the dark slash of the terrace railing that bracketed the sprawled figure of Mrs. Lavington and the pool of blood. Against the white of the snow, it looked like a dark blot on a clean page of paper. The single set of footprints to her body were tiny dark imprints in the sheet of white covering the terrace. That pool of blood was disturbing, so I shifted my attention away from the images to the neat rows and columns.

"I find having it all spread out helps me organize my thoughts." Vogel nodded at the board. "I listed everything I've confirmed about the movements of Mrs. Lavington's acquaintances. All the notes you see there have been confirmed by at least two witnesses."

"How ingenious." We sat in silence a few moments as I scanned the complex chart. "I see you have Mrs. Ashford returning to her chalet before Mrs. Lavington's death, but there's a question mark as well."

"She had a telegram delivered late, someone dropping out of the upcoming ski race. One of the hotel staff took it to the chalet at about half ten, which lessens the possibility Mrs. Ashford was involved. It's a walk of five to ten minutes back to the hotel when the path is clear. With fresh snow and icy conditions, it takes longer."

"Although she had a good reason to be upset with Mrs. Lavington. Mr. Rimington told me something about the death of her son. Have you learned about that?"

"Only that he died in"—he inched his chair closer to the desk and checked his notebook—"1921. A motor accident, but I don't have the details from the English police yet."

"It was Mrs. Lavington who was driving." I relayed what Jasper had told me.

Vogel picked up a pencil and made notes as I spoke, then studied the board over my shoulder. "So Mrs. Ashford has a strong motive." He rolled the pencil between his palms. "On one hand, we have Mr. Klein, who didn't have the opportunity to harm Mrs. Lavington. While on the other hand, we have Mrs. Ashford, who might just possibly have had time to return to the hotel after receiving the telegram. But why would she wait several years to exact revenge?"

"Perhaps this was the perfect opportunity."

"You're thinking of the conversation you overheard on the train," Vogel said.

"Yes. If Mrs. Lavington's death looked like an accident, no one would connect it with her son's death several years prior. Could it have been Mrs. Ashford who was blackmailing Mrs. Lavington?"

Vogel's head bobbed in tiny nods. "My thoughts were tracing along that same route. I need to find that typewriter. It will be challenging to connect the blackmailer to Mrs. Lavington without it. Even though the staff said no one had borrowed the hotel's typewriter, I had a look. It's an Underwood. The note was typed on a Remington Portable, so no luck there. There aren't many other places here in St. Moritz where a guest would have access to a typewriter. Of course, the blackmailer could have typed it up at home and brought it with them, which would make locating it much more difficult."

He pushed back his chair and swung one knee over the other. "Have any other details come to light about the other guests?"

"Yes, I spoke to the Grogans separately. Apparently, Mrs. Lavington's plans would have run the millinery into the ground. According to both Hattie and Rob, that was the case. It seems Hattie was determined to become the sole owner of the business. She was willing to buy out Mrs. Lavington, even if it cost quite a lot. Rob was adamant that his wife was better off with Mrs. Lavington out of the business. He's certainly not broken up about her death. Actually, neither one of them were."

"A financial motive." Vogel went around the desk and added a new list to the right side of the board.

Revenge—Fredrick Klein, Etta Morgan, Amy Ashford
Financial gain—Hattie and Rob Grogan

He tossed the chalk into the tray. "So we have two possible motives—revenge, in the case of three people, and a financial motive for two others." He brushed his hands together, dusting his fingers. "But the problem remains, if any of these people met Mrs. Lavington on the terrace, levitation must have been involved." He thumped the photograph of the terrace with the knuckle of his index finger.

"Could someone have stepped inside her footprints?"

He returned to the desk and handed me a folder with photographs. They were close-up images of the footprints, which clearly showed it was a woman's footprint, a triangular shape where the ball of the foot touched, and then a smaller square mark behind it where the heel had broken the snow. A ruler had been laid alongside the print.

Vogel dropped back into his swivel chair. "Mrs. Lavington had small dainty feet. I've checked the shoe sizes of Mrs. Grogan, Mrs. Ashford, and Miss Morgan against the measurements of the imprint. They're all too large." He tilted his head, indicating the board behind me.

"Ah, that explains the list of women's names with numbers beside them."

"All of the ladies wear a size shoe larger than Mrs. Lavington's. If any one of them had stepped inside the footprints, the imprints in the snow would have been bigger." He rubbed his hand over his triangular beard. "Yet again, I have another negative clue."

I handed the photos back. "It's progress—of a sort."

"You might say that." With his shoulders drooping, Vogel looked quite glum.

I twisted around to study the photographs taped to the blackboard that showed the whole scene again, ignoring the spill of blood as best I could. The little table beside Mrs. Lavington was empty. I inched my chair closer for a better look, then I swiveled the back to the korporale. "The money."

"I'm sorry?"

"The note that Etta found indicated Mrs. Lavington had received instructions about where to take the next installment of the money. It must have been to the terrace that evening. I noticed Mrs. Lavington glanced at the clock a few times. She left a few minutes before ten, which must have been the time she was to meet the blackmailer."

"But several people, including you, reported she was tired—yawning, in fact."

"I remember that too, but I bet she had the money with her, probably in her handbag, and she was supposed to take it to the terrace. Why would she go to the terrace when she was already sleepy unless she had to? Mrs. Lavington told me that in the past, the drop-off instructions had always been to put the money in an envelope inside a newspaper and then go to certain place in a park where she was to sit on a bench. She'd always been instructed to leave the money. Perhaps she'd been told to leave the money on the terrace. No envelope or newspaper were found?"

"No, nothing like that, only her handbag, which contained typical items—nail file, comb, compact, lipstick, and a handkerchief."

In the pictures, the wood on the table was a dark circle

against the white background of snow that covered the terrace. I jumped up and went to the blackboard. "Look, there's no snow on the table. What would be more natural than to brush the snow off of the table before putting an envelope or newspaper down?"

Vogel picked up his pencil and tapped a quick beat on the wooden desktop, his abstracted gaze on the blackboard. "So Mrs. Lavington met with her blackmailer, and that person took the money away, leaving Mrs. Lavington alive." The tapping stopped a moment, then resumed. "Or the blackmailer and the murderer are one and the same."

The glass in the door rattled as someone tapped on the frame. Oberwaller opened the door and stuck his head in. "You asked me to remind you of your meeting in a quarter hour, sir."

Vogel stood. "Right. Thank you, Oberwaller."

I picked up my handbag and hooked it over my wrist, studying the grid on the blackboard for a final time as I moved around my chair. "Who is Mr. Tobinn?" The name was unfamiliar, and the row which would have tracked his movements throughout the evening was blank.

"He booked a room at the hotel." Vogel slipped one arm into his coat and turned the page of his notebook with the other, then read aloud, "A Mr. Galen V. Tobinn reserved the middle room on the top floor at the back of the hotel—the one that was unoccupied." He shrugged into the wool coat and adjusted the lapels. "The next morning he contacted the hotel. He said he'd been delayed and canceled the two days remaining on his reservation. Do you know him?"

"No, I don't."

Vogel tucked the notebook into a pocket, then locked the folder with the pictures in a desk drawer. "I'm trying to track him down as well, but so far nothing from the British authorities. I have a request in to track the telegram that canceled the reservation too, but so far no news. Tobinn made his reservation through Cook's a week prior to the incident." He held his office door open. "Thank you again for taking time away from your holiday, Miss Belgrave, to provide some additional insight into Mrs. Lavington's friends and acquaintances. I greatly appreciate your help. I hope you're able to put this sad situation out of your mind and enjoy the rest of your time here."

I'd been about to step across the threshold, but I turned back to him. "But we'll speak again soon, I'm sure."

The corners of his mouth turned down as he made a little negative shake of the head. "There will be no need. I won't trouble you further. You've already missed out on your time in the Alps. I can't continue to monopolize your time."

"But the case isn't solved."

"No, but you've done all I've asked. You've spoken to the people involved and shared the information you gleaned with me. And," he waved his hand at the photographs on the chalkboard, "I appreciate your insights. All very helpful. There's nothing more you can do."

"No, there's also—"

"I'm sorry, but I must leave now." He gestured to the door.

I clamped down on the argument that was bubbling up. He wouldn't listen. Not at this moment.

I said goodbye and left. How could he think I could put aside all the questions around Mrs. Lavington's death and go about a carefree holiday? That wasn't possible. Some people might be able to do it, but not me. Whether or not Vogel thought I was off the case didn't matter. I was still on it.

CHAPTER 22

*W*hen I returned to the hotel, I found a note from Juliet. It read, *I have a pair of skis you can borrow. Come to the chalet, and I'll outfit you. The desk clerk can tell you how to get here.*

I followed the directions from the clerk and went out the front doors of the hotel, around the restaurant, and began the steep climb up the hill where Jasper and I had met Mr. Lavington earlier. I passed the retaining wall that ran from the sun terrace down to the lane. I couldn't see anyone, but the hum of conversation floated down to me as I strode up the incline.

I trudged along the firmly packed snow. When I reached a plateau, which was high enough to give a view of the hotel, I paused to draw in a deep breath. I turned, hands on hips, and surveyed the sunbathers with rolled shirtsleeves on the terrace, basking in the sunshine.

The rock wall fell away from the terrace in a sheer drop. Snow clung to a few of the grooves between the stones, but the tiny patches of white were sparse. Because of the lack of snow, someone with climbing experience could have scaled it on the night Mrs. Lavington died without leaving any sign of their movements. But if someone had gained the terrace by the wall, how did they get to Mrs. Lavington without leaving a trace?

I trod on, mulling over the problem. The road stayed level, and the going was much easier as the path curved through a dense area of snow-laden pines. I passed the signpost Mr. Lavington had pointed out earlier and kept walking.

The lane branched out now and again into smaller lanes dotted with chalets. I followed the wooden sign pointing up a faint trail through the snow and came out of the evergreens into a small clearing with two chalets situated on a ridge facing the lake. They were darling little cottages with empty window boxes, which I was sure in the summer would overflow with flowers. For now, the only decorations were the diamond patterns cut in the thick wood of the window boxes and the balcony that ran across the front of the house.

I went up the path to the far chalet. As I approached, I recognized the figure striding down a different trail coming toward me. Mrs. Ashford wore a pair of trousers, a hip-length wool coat, a wide-brimmed hat, and sturdy boots. A coil of rope hung on one shoulder. She loped along at a jaunty pace, using her ice axe as a walking stick. She held the metal axe portion of the waist-high stick loosely, similar to the way Jasper wielded his walking stick when we were out for a stroll around London. Mrs. Ashford hadn't seen me yet, and I paused to wait for her.

She came to a section of the path that dropped down a miniature bluff a few yards high. Without breaking stride, she dug the end of the stick opposite the axe head into the ground and gripped the flat metal portion of the axe head. She didn't break her stride as she used the ice axe to steady herself over the rough slope, then continued on. She waved when she spotted me. "Miss Belgrave, isn't it?" she asked as she reached me.

"Yes, that's right. Good afternoon, Mrs. Ashford. I'm supposed to meet Juliet here."

"She'll be along shortly, I'm sure." Mrs. Ashford led the way up the path to the chalet and opened the unlocked door. "Do come in."

Beyond the short entry hall, the chalet had a snug little sitting room and the kitchen on the main floor. A staircase at the back led to a balcony, where I could see two bedrooms and a bath between them.

Mrs. Ashford propped the ice axe near the door, then hooked the coiled rope on a peg along with her coat and hat. As she took my coat and hung it up, she said, "Juliet had a meeting with a rather verbose individual, let's say." She smiled, exposing her toothy grin, and waved me into the sitting room. Unlike the hotel, which kept the interior rooms toasty, it was cool inside the chalet, but if Mrs. Ashford and Juliet had both been out all morning, the chill was understandable. I crossed my arms and wished I'd kept my coat on.

Mrs. Ashford crossed the sitting room, her nailed boots clicking across the hardwood. "Let me tidy up." Moving quickly, she gathered up a stack of books, notepads, magazines, and newspapers from the sofa. "There you are." She indicated the sofa with a tilt of her head. "As you can see, I do need a secretary." She lifted the stack of reading material, her tone good-natured. "Juliet is very tidy. I'm quite a trial to her." Mrs. Ashford dumped everything onto the corner of the desk by the window. The rooftops of St. Moritz filled in the valley below, and beyond the buildings the silver of the lake spread out along the valley. The mountains on the far side of the lake were darker than usual because of the shadows cast from the clouds above them.

Mrs. Ashford moved the fire guard and knelt on the hearth. She struck a match and lit a fire that had already been laid. I scooted nearer the flames.

Mrs. Ashford plopped down in the chair across from me. "Just let me get these boots off—I'm still breaking them in, and I've had about all I can stand of them—then I'll make us some tea."

"That would be lovely." Never in a million years would I have taken off my shoes when I had a guest, but I could certainly sympathize with aching feet. I settled back against the cushions on the end of the sofa nearest the fire.

Two photographs in travel frames were propped up on the end table. The first was of a much younger Mrs. Ashford and a tall man with a mustache and luxurious sideburns that had been popular decades ago. The two of them stood on a rocky ridge, both gripping ice axes and leaning slightly toward each other. A range of mountain peaks filled the background. Her deceased husband, I assumed. The other photograph was of a young man in uniform with a serious expression on his smooth face. His hooded eyes resembled Mrs. Ashford's, and I wondered if he'd also had his mother's toothy grin when he smiled.

Mrs. Ashford looked up from loosening her bootlaces and noticed my interest in the photos. "My husband and I in the French Alps, and my son, Howard. He died after the war."

There was no bitterness or anger in her words, only a sort of wistful regret. "I'm sorry to hear that," I said.

She worked one boot off and began on the second. "Your Mr. Rimington reminds me of Howard."

"Oh, he's not my Mr. Rimington."

She removed the other boot. "Oh, I think he is. It's plain to see."

"Well, perhaps." I couldn't help smiling a bit.

She tucked the laces into the boots, her movements slowing. "I think Howard might have been something like Mr. Rimington. Howard had a lightness to him, an easy-going manner, the same as Mr. Rimington." She drew in a long breath. "It must be the questions from the korporale that have stirred up my memories. Grief is such an unpredictable thing. I go along—not fine, but reconciled to the situation. Then, up from nowhere, a memory hits, rather like a lightning strike, and my sorrow has me by the throat again, barely able to breathe." She pressed her hands to the arm of the chair to stand. "But I'm sure grief has touched your life too. So few people have escaped it, with the war and the flu."

"My cousin survived the war, but his mind is . . . different."

Her arms relaxed. "Which brings a different kind of grief."

I'd probably never have another opening like this, so even though I was cringing on the inside, I said, "May I ask a very impertinent question?"

"I doubt you'll shock me." Her toothy grin appeared. "I'm what they call *unconventional*. Go ahead."

"I suppose you know Korporale Vogel is looking into Mrs. Lavington's death?"

She subsided back into the chair, her face serious. "Yes, I gathered that from the questions he asked me about my movements. I suppose that as a lady detective, you've learned of the connection between Howard and Mrs. Lavington." I nodded, and she gave a little bob of her head, then looked out the window to the mountain view. "And you probably also know I considered making Mrs. Lavington pay for her actions through a lawsuit."

"Yes, I did wonder about that."

She looked back at me. "I'll be entirely honest with you, Miss Belgrave, because I like you. I can't help but like women who take on the unusual roles, push the boundaries out for the others who will come along behind them." Mrs. Ashford straightened her spine, and I had the feeling that if there were a Bible nearby she would have taken it up and put her hand on it. "I did want Mrs. Lavington to pay. I was very angry for a long while, but then . . . well, *vengeance belongeth unto me*. Do you know that verse?"

"*I will recompense, saith the Lord*. My father was a vicar."

"Ah, and you were attentive. Many young people have rejected faith today. I understand. After the war . . . well, I understand. I truly do. But once I began to think on that verse," Mrs. Ashford's shoulders lifted, and she spread her hands, "it isn't for me to mete out punishment. I decided to leave it and get on with the things I enjoyed." She lifted her eyebrows and threw a glance at the window. "Like climbing. Despite everything, the mountains still bring me joy. I decided to concentrate on joy, not revenge. Does that answer your question?"

"I believe so." And I did believe Mrs. Ashford. It was obvious that her grief was still raw at times, but she was so sincere and open that I found it hard to picture her carrying out a methodical plot for vengeance and then being able to speak about focusing on joy. Was she that good of an actress? Was anyone that good of an actress? Would Miss Ravenna have been able to pull off that sort of performance with murderous thoughts inside her?

The door creaked, and cold air whipped into the room, chilling the back of my neck. "So sorry I'm late, Olive," Juliet said, shattering the confiding atmosphere. "I forgot what a windbag old—er—but you're not interested in that. Let's get you ready to ski. Come along, I have an extra pair of skis that will be perfect for you . . ."

Juliet said, "The most important thing you need to know is how to stop."

"I agree." A frigid breeze stirred the conifers, and several great slabs of snow fell to the ground with soft thuds. The gray clouds had multiplied. They were drifting down from the mountain, tinging the day with a strange gray backwash that covered half the valley. Juliet and I were still in the sun, but we'd both agreed a shorter lesson would be best since the weather was turning. "Stopping, yes. A critical skill I must know. I agree wholeheartedly."

"Right." She angled the front of her skis toward each other. "So you turn your heels out and bring the tips of your skis close to each other, like this in a V shape, but don't cross them. Then you use your weight and the position of your body to regulate your speed and direction. To slow yourself down and stop, keep your weight over the center of your skis and widen the back of the V." She demonstrated gliding down the gentle slope. She rotated her heels slightly, pushing the back of her skis farther apart, and coasted to a stop on a flat meadow-like area a few feet away. She shouted over her shoulder, "Don't use your ski poles, just bend your knees and lean forward a touch to get yourself moving. Give it a try!"

I settled into the stance, the wind whipping at my skirt hem. I was glad I'd worn my thickest wool tights. Juliet wore breeches and thick socks with her calf-high boots. I hadn't thought to pack breeches. I wished I had, but I didn't realize that women's fashion was so practical when it came to skiing.

I tried my best to replicate Juliet's actions, but seconds after I began moving, the space between the tips of my skis widened. One leg juddered out over the snow, jerking away, and suddenly I was lying in the snow, skis, poles, and legs tangled, looking at the treetops and gunmetal-gray clouds. I scrambled up, and Juliet shouted, "Not bad for a first try."

"Really? I thought that was rubbish."

"Nonsense. One does a lot of falling at first, but then it'll click. It will be worth it. I promise. It's the best feeling in the world to swish back and forth across the snow. Once you've mastered stopping, we'll work on turns."

"Let's not get ahead of ourselves." I ignored the dusting of flakes working their way below my collar and down my spine. "I'm only here for a few more days." I gripped the ski poles tighter and gave it another go.

After about a quarter of an hour, we'd worked our way down the hill, and I'd managed to stay upright for most of it. Then we sidestepped our way back up the hill and repeated the process several times. At the end of a half hour, I could actually stay on my feet for most of the distance. It was a pitifully short distance, but I was able to navigate it without pitching into the snow. I was flushed and perspiring as if I'd run a marathon, and I regretted my woolen layers. Juliet looked cool and stylish and wasn't even breathing hard.

She eyed the clouds and their shadows, which now completely curtained the far side of the valley and most of the lake. We were still in the sun, but the steely-gray layer was approaching, casting a veil over the valley. "You've done very well. Next time we'll work on turns. And then you'll be ready to go up higher."

"Perhaps give me a day or two to recover. I think I'll need it."

"Skiing is fatiguing, but it does keep one fit." She pointed with one of her poles to a trail through the trees. Narrow tracks indicated several people had skied along it since the last snowfall. "Let's head back that way. After this belt of trees, take the fork to the left. It'll bring us out right by the chalet. Don't turn right. It goes to a gorgeous slope, but the side of it drops off to the Immergrüne Valley."

"Left fork it is. I'm definitely done for today."

"Would you like to stop in at the chalet for a cup of tea?"

"That would be heavenly." Especially since I hadn't gotten the cup of tea Mrs. Ashford had offered earlier. Juliet had been so keen to get me outfitted with skis and get to the mountain that the tea had been forgotten.

I managed to make it to the chalet, only falling twice.

Once I'd taken the skis off, my legs felt a thousand times lighter, although they were rubbery after all the effort I'd put in. I propped the skis outside the chalet alongside Juliet's. I stabbed my poles into the snow and tilted the handles toward the wooden bar, as Juliet had done. It seemed the area had been constructed as a collection point for ski gear.

"Hello? Amy?" Juliet called as she paused in the entry of the chalet to unbutton her coat. I followed her in and shut the door. "She must've gone down to the village."

I was disappointed. I'd hoped to continue the discussion with Mrs. Ashford about her son. However, off the top of my head I couldn't think of an easy way to turn the conversation to his death and how it linked up with Mrs. Lavington. Every opening I'd thought of on the trudge back to the chalet sounded gauche and rude, so perhaps it was fortuitous that she was out.

Juliet stuffed her gloves in her coat pocket and unwound her scarf from her neck. "Amy said she might go—"

Metal pinged as a medallion on a chain hit the hardwood floor. Juliet stepped back and looked around her feet. "I must get the catch on my necklace fixed. That's the second time it's caught on my scarf and I've pulled it off."

"Here it is, under the bench. How pretty." The gold octagonal pendant had the letter *J* engraved on it. A decorative vine intertwined around the stem of the letter in two loops. The pendant was still on the chain, and I handed it to her, letting the tiny links of gold puddle into her palm.

"Thank you." She dropped it into the pocket of her breeches, then hooked her scarf on the row of pegs above the bench by the door. I followed suit as she gestured to the sitting room. "Make yourself comfortable. I'll be back in a moment with the tea." She disappeared through the doorway. The clink of crockery came from the kitchen as I strolled around the room. I was afraid if I sat down I might drift off immediately. *Tired* didn't begin to capture how I felt. *Completely knackered* was much more accurate, but I also had that pleasantly lethargic and somewhat smug feeling that comes after exercise.

But then my steps quickened, and I forgot my fatigue. I was drawn like a metal filing to magnet and crossed to the little desk positioned by the windows. A typewriter sat in the center of it, between a stack of books and papers on one side and a clipboard on the other. I hadn't seen it earlier because Mrs. Ashford had put the stack she'd gathered up from the sofa on the desk, blocking the typewriter from my view when I sat on the sofa. Now that I'd moved around to the other side of the room, it was the first thing I noticed about the desk.

I nudged the stack to the side, exposing the bright lettering on the typewriter, which read, *Remington Portable*.

On the other side of the desk was a clipboard with typed pages fastened under the metal bracket. I picked it up. The heading ran, *Ashford Ski Cup Challenge*. A date later in the week was centered on the next line. Columns of names, numbers, and times filled the rest of the page.

I glanced over my shoulder at the kitchen, but Juliet was out of sight. The clatter of dishes and the soft thump of cupboard doors indicated she was still busy with the tea tray. I stepped around the desk, closer to the window. The light had changed with the approaching storm to a muted bluish-gray, but it was still bright enough that I could easily see every typed zero had a tiny blank space, a diagonal slash through the ink of the oval. I had a quick look at the pages under the top one, but there were only more lists of names. A whistle shrilled, and I jumped as if a firecracker had gone off beside me. The teapot, I realized.

I replaced the clipboard. An unused pile of paper sat at the back of the desk, and I flicked through it, but it was all pristine and as white as the snow outside. I stepped back to move away, but then I saw the rubbish bin under the desk, which contained a few carbons.

I snatched the carbons out and held the back sides up to the light. They'd been used more than once, and many of the typewritten lines crossed over each other, but some of the key strikes were visible and not overridden. I was able to read them despite seeing them in the reverse. I flicked through the carbons, stopping at the third or fourth one, which was something about funding for the Ladies' Winter Sporting Association. The pound sign showed up in three places on the page. It didn't sit evenly on the lines. Instead, it was tilted slightly backward, away from the numbers, like the pound sign on the note Etta had brought to me, except in the reverse direction, which made sense because I was looking at the reverse side of the imprint.

A floorboard creaked. A jittery tingle of adrenaline zinged through me at the thought of being caught snooping. I folded the carbon, inky side inward, then folded it again into a little square and slipped it into my skirt pocket. I called out, "I see you have a Remington Portable," as I moved away from the desk.

Julia raised her voice from the kitchen. "Yes. Quite handy. I use it for the association's business."

"I see. Does Mrs. Ashford ever use it?"

Juliet came back into the room, cups clinking on the tray she carried. "Gracious, no. That's why she hired me. She's *all thumbs*, as she says, when it comes to touch-typing."

But I was sure Mrs. Ashford could pick a few lines with one or two fingers if she wanted to.

"Why do you ask?" Juliet put the tray down on the table in front of the sofa. "If you don't mind pouring, I'll stir up the fire."

I sat down, glad to have something to do. "I'm learning to touch-type. I'm dreadfully slow, but my accuracy is improving."

"Yes, that's half the battle." Juliet removed the fire guard and poked the fire before adding some logs to it. Since her back was to me, I took a deep, yet silent, breath to calm my heart rate, which was galloping along as it had during the most strenuous bits of my ski lesson. I'd drink a cup of tea and then make my excuses. It would be perfectly natural to be exhausted and return to the hotel after trying to master the tricky art of skiing.

Juliet sat back on her heels and watched the fire for a moment, then she swiveled around. She settled on the floor, angling her feet to one side as she leaned against one of the upholstered chairs that flanked the fireplace.

I handed her a teacup. Her glance lingered on my fingers as she accepted it. It was only then that I noticed a black smudge on my thumb.

CHAPTER 23

*J*uliet's gaze zipped over to the desk and back to my blackened thumb.

"I—um—" Why hadn't I offered to rekindle the fire? Soot would have been the perfect excuse for inky-looking fingers, but words failed me as Juliet's eyes narrowed.

"I'm curious about something, Olive," she said, after taking a sip of her tea. "Perhaps you'll indulge me. When I saw Emmaline come out of your compartment on the train, I couldn't help but wonder why she was there. You weren't friends—not even acquaintances. Do you know what I think? I think Emmaline wanted to talk to the lady detective in private."

That certainly wasn't what I thought she'd say, but I would rather talk about the train than my smudged fingers. "We just had a short chat."

Still holding her teacup, Juliet shifted her weight. She tucked her feet under her body and stood in one lithe motion, then walked over to the desk. With her back to me, she said, "I think Emmaline asked for help with a little . . . problem, let's call it." Juliet picked up the clipboard, scanned it, then returned it to the desk. "A troublesome issue involving blackmail, wasn't it?"

"What we discussed was private."

Juliet didn't seem to hear me. She put her tea on top of the clipboard, then braced her hands on the back of her hips. Elbows out, head down, she took a few steps away from the desk. "I believe you may be able to help me. I'm in a bit of a sticky situation myself. Since I've been foolish enough to invite you inside for tea, I see that I've inadvertently made it worse."

I put down my own cup of tea, mentally measuring the distance to the door. If I dived around the sofa, I could probably make it outside, even if she darted at me and tried to block my way.

But Juliet wasn't even looking at me. Head still down, hands on her hips, elbows still flared out, she paced back the other way. "I knew Emmaline for years. She could be quite fun, but she could also be a *beastly* pain. When she married Ben, she decided I wasn't posh enough. She cut me from her group. I was hurt and feeling a little vengeful."

Oh my. This was not a conversation I wanted to be having in an isolated chalet. Juliet didn't seem to sense my wariness. She was busy tracking back and forth, looking fixedly at the floorboards. "It's no secret there was no love lost between us. Emmaline was not a kind person. She used people. She didn't love Ben. She married him because she saw an opportunity to move up in the world. His family tree goes back to the Wars of the Roses, you know. And with his sachet of being a climber—well, it was perfect for her, social climber that she was." She gave a little mirthless laugh. "That's quite a good pun, if I do say so myself."

I stood and took a few steps toward the door. With my tired legs, I felt as if I were moving through waist-deep water in a swimming pool. "I'm afraid I must leave—"

Juliet didn't seem to hear me. She was completely lost in her memories. She paused at the window and looked out. "Emmaline's new friends, the ones she made after her marriage, didn't know her when she was younger. I was one of the few people who did, and that gave me a little knowledge. I decided to put it to use . . ."

I took a few more steps to the door. "What sort of knowledge?"

She turned toward me and crossed her arms. The grayish light from the windows created a murky silhouette of her figure. "Of her true age."

I was halfway around the sofa now, but I halted. "I'm not sure I follow."

Juliet began to pace again, the heels of her boots cracking against the wooden floor. "The age difference between Emmaline and Ben is six years."

My unease began to drain way. "That is a bit of a gap."

"Yes, but it's especially significant when it's the woman who's older. You see, Emmaline lied to Ben about her age." Arms still crossed, Juliet leaned toward me as she said, "She told Ben she was a year *younger* than he was. Since she'd been so rotten to me, I couldn't help using that detail to gouge her just a teeny bit and make her life a shade more difficult." Juliet straightened, turned back to the window, and ran her hand along the wooden casement. "I typed up a letter and sent it to her, telling her she had to bring five pounds to the park and leave it on the bench or I'd tell her husband her true age." She gave a little vibration of her head, her words infused with pride as if she'd pulled off a difficult conjuring trick.

I was speechless for a moment, and then I found my voice. "You can't be serious." I couldn't keep the slight laugh out of my words.

"Oh, I am. Completely serious. Emmaline was incredibly sensitive about the age difference. I teased her about it once when they first became engaged. It was Ben's birthday, and I said wasn't it just the caterpillar's kimono that she'd caught a bloke who didn't care that she was older. Her reaction was—well, she was a frightful harpy about it."

It did seem like a small thing—especially compared to secrets that usually were at the root of blackmail, but I had to concede that Emmaline had been right. If a wife was older than her husband, it could be fodder for society gossip. But something else bothered me. "How could anyone—especially her fiancé—not know her true birthdate?"

Juliet shoved her hands into her breeches pockets and leaned against the windowsill. "Her father was in the foreign service. Emmaline was born in India, and there's no coordination of birth records across the empire, apparently. She had some sort of fever when she was a few years old. When she was well enough to make the sea voyage, she and her mother traveled to England—or at least that's the story she always told. I lived in the same village. We were the same age."

She lifted her shoulders. "When one is six, there are no secrets about one's age. Over the years, Emmaline picked up new acquaintances and dropped most of her friends from those early years, except for me. By the time she met Ben, her mother and father had died. By the time we were eighteen, Emmaline didn't have any friends of long-standing. I lost touch with her for a few years during the war, but we reconnected afterward. When we met up again, she'd shaved several years off of her age, which I thought was silly. Being squeamish about one's age is utter foolishness, of course, but it mattered to her. After she behaved so badly to me and cut me, it gave me no end of delight to goad her about it. I realize now it was incredibly rash and shortsighted of me, but it gave me such a wonderful sense of satisfaction to know she was fretting over it."

"So you sent her blackmail notes when you were in England around the holidays at Easter and Christmas and then again during the summer."

She pushed off from the windowsill. "Yes, how did you know I traveled then?" Before I could answer, she said, "Oh, Emmaline told you *when* she received the notes. I see. How astute of you to pick up on those details. That was sloppy of me, not to realize I was creating a pattern. But, in any case, it was just a foolish prank."

"I'm afraid the police won't look on it that way."

She held out her flattened hand, palm up. "Exactly. You see my problem. I knew you would. That's why I've confided in you, Olive. If I admit I was blackmailing Emmaline, they'll think I killed her, and I didn't." She clasped her hands together in a pleading attitude. "I swear I didn't."

"But you did send her a blackmail note on the train

and then later sent her instructions to take the money to the sun terrace?"

Juliet sighed, her hands dropping to her sides. "Yes. Emmaline should have left it on the terrace, and I would have been able to retrieve it with no one being the wiser, but then my dratted sleeve caught fire, and I couldn't get away."

"I don't see many options open to you at this point. The best thing to do is to tell the police everything."

"I'm certainly *not* doing that."

Why did no one want to talk to the police? First Etta and now Juliet. It wasn't even officially a murder inquiry, just an investigation of an accident. And on top of that, Vogel was the most agreeable police official I'd ever dealt with. "I'm sure Korporale Vogel will hear you out without jumping to conclusions."

Juliet came across the room and lunged knees-first onto the sofa. She clutched the back of the sofa. "Please help me sort this out. Emmaline is gone. She's no longer your client. I want to hire you to take care of this tricky situation. That's what you do, isn't it? Help people when they become entangled in something like this?"

"I can't say that I've ever had a blackmailer as a client. It's a cut-and-dried sort of thing. Not much wiggle room there, I'm afraid."

She scowled. "Well, I'm not going to the police."

A movement out the window behind her caught my eye. "It seems they've come to you."

She twisted around and followed the direction of my gaze to the area at the side of the cottage, where Vogel had paused to examine the skis and poles before continuing up the path to the door.

CHAPTER 24

*L*ater that evening Jasper waited until our dessert plates had been removed and the attendant had left our table before he asked, "And what brought Vogel to the chalet?"

"He remembered Juliet was secretary for the ladies' sport association, which meant she might have a typewriter. He clocked it as soon as he walked in and asked if he could have a look. That put paid to Juliet's idea that she wouldn't tell the police about her—um—notes," I improvised, mindful that we were in a crowded dining room.

The rest of our dinner companions had left the table, but Jasper and I were lingering over pudding, discussing our day. Jasper's update had been concise. "After our walk, I spent the rest of the day hunched over the desk in my room," he'd said. "I'm nearly done. Tell me about your day, old bean. It must be considerably more interesting than mine."

It had certainly taken more time for me to share details of my day. I'd described my encounter with Etta,

Vogel's blackboard, the ski lesson, and then my discovery of the carbons. I sipped my coffee, then, keeping my voice low, I said, "Juliet swore she had nothing to do with Mrs. Lavington's death. I believe everyone here—at least everyone in our little circle of acquaintances here in Alpine House—has realized that the police are suspicious and are investigating to see if the death was more than an accident. Juliet was adamant she didn't harm Mrs. Lavington, and I believed her. And she didn't leave the lounge, so there's no way she could have been involved."

"So the blackmail wasn't related to Mrs. Lavington's death?"

"No, it looks as if it was completely separate. Just a spurned friend getting revenge on someone who hurt her."

"Rather odd, that. Most people don't resort to blackmail in that situation."

"I agree, but I suppose Juliet never thought she'd get caught. She called it a prank."

"I'll wager Vogel didn't view it so lightly."

"No, he didn't. He was quite stern with her. Well, as stern as someone with an amiable disposition can be." Jasper had been leaning close to hear my quiet words, but he pulled back and looked down into his coffee cup.

He asked, "Is Juliet in police custody?"

"No. Apparently, Vogel decided not to take any action about the blackmail. Not yet, at any rate. He warned Juliet that she could be in *boiling water*, as he phrased it, but didn't take her to the station."

"Boiling water?"

"Vogel likes to pepper his conversation with English expressions, but they're not always used accurately."

"And do you correct him when his word choice is off?"

"Yes, he asked me to."

Jasper went quiet again and rearranged the position of his dessert fork on his plate. "So you and Vogel," Jasper paused and swallowed as an expression traced across his face as if he had eaten something that had gone off, "think it's possible that the murderer took advantage of the fact that Mrs. Lavington was on the terrace?"

"Yes, although, as Vogel says, levitation must have been involved. The only footprints on the terrace belonged to Mrs. Lavington. No one came down from above because no snow on the railings of the balconies was disturbed. The snow on the roof and on the ground surrounding the terrace was unmarred as well."

"Essentially, you have an impossible crime. If you figure out how it was committed, then most likely you'll have your *who* along with your *how-done-it.*"

"Yes, if we can get that far. It's like a conundrum out of one of your crime books."

Jasper ran his thumb around the rim of his coffee cup. With his attention focused on it, he said, "Vogel seems to be a good chap, if a little shorthanded."

"I suppose that's true, but he didn't endear himself to me today."

Jasper looked up quickly. "What happened?"

"He basically dismissed me from the case."

The corners of Jasper's mouth turned up in a grin. "I would've liked to have seen your reaction to that."

"I'll have you know that I didn't argue or behave in an unbecoming way. Korporale Vogel was on his way out of the office to meet with some officials when it came up. I decided on retreat instead of confrontation."

"I'm sure your behavior was exemplary—at least outwardly—but I also know the thought of leaving something unfinished is reprehensible to you."

"Yes, I do find it extremely aggravating."

Jasper picked up his spoon and plunged it into his parfait. "So Vogel isn't in favor any longer?"

"Oh, I suppose he's a good egg overall, but I can't see why he's shown me the door. Literally! He thanked me for my help with a case and told me to enjoy the rest of my holiday."

"Maybe he thinks you might want some time in the mountains that doesn't involve thinking about Mrs. Lavington's death."

I pushed my coffee cup away. "Even if I wanted to do that, I wouldn't be able to. I couldn't put it totally out of my mind. It would always be in the back corner of my thoughts, like the dripping of a tap in the middle of the night."

"Yes, quite annoying, those sort of things . . ." Jasper put down his spoon, then rotated his coffee cup. I sensed there was something he wanted to say to me. He drew a breath, sat up a bit straighter, then subsided back into his chair as the waiter approached, holding a coffeepot.

Once the waiter left our table, I scooted my chair closer. "What is it?"

"Nothing important."

I reached across the table and caught his hand. "Jasper, something's bothering you. I can tell. Please share it." He began to shake his head, but before he could brush the topic away, I gave his hand a little shake. "Don't deny it. I know you."

A quick grin flashed across his face. "So you do." He grimaced. "I'm afraid it puts me in a very bad light."

"I doubt that." I raised my eyebrows and gave a little *go-ahead* nod.

"All right, then." He concentrated on brushing a crumb off the tablecloth with his free hand. "I've got a little devil sitting on my shoulder, whispering things in my ear. A little green-eyed monster."

"You mean jealousy? You're jealous of someone . . ."

He released my hand and brushed his hair off his forehead. His wavy locks refused to conform to the current style and stay slicked back from his face. "Well, now I've gone and done it. Let the truth slip out. I shouldn't have had that brandy." He grinned and spoke to the tablecloth again. "This holiday hasn't gone as I planned. When I invited you to come on this trip, I thought my project would be wrapped up quickly, and then we'd have an enjoyable break. Instead, I've spent almost every day locked away in my room."

"But I understand. What you're doing is important."

"You've been a brick about it."

"What does that have to do with jealousy?"

"While I'm shuttered away upstairs, you're working closely with Vogel to sort out what happened with Mrs. Lavington. I know how much you enjoy sorting out answers to problems like that. Vogel is a charming and handsome fellow . . . and, well, he has a crime board contraption. A murder board, if you will. I'm sadly lacking in murder boards. Hard for a chap to compete with something like that—in your case, I mean. I know how fond you are of resolving those pesky details around a crime."

"I do become rather single-minded—"

Jasper went on as if now that he'd started talking he wanted to get it all out. "I've been feeling resentful of him for the last few days, but I didn't want to admit it to myself." His grip on my fingers tightened. "But when you said he'd showed you to the door, I felt a wonderful sense of satisfaction that you wouldn't be around him anymore. Then it hit me—I'm jealous of the bloke. I suppose I was worried that perhaps you might be . . . oh, I don't know . . . attracted to the fellow, let's say."

"Vogel? He's rather old, you know."

Jasper laughed, a sharp, quick burst of mirth that caused a few of the diners to look toward our table. He sobered. "As am I, compared to you."

"Vogel is *years* older than you. But if you're really worried about age gaps, you're only a few years older than me. It's not at all like the gap between Mr. and Mrs. Lavington. Besides, the disapproval about age gaps is all bosh anyway. Who cares if Mrs. Lavington was older than her husband? Who cares if there's a few years difference between us? Society and its rules cause no end of bother. I know you put on the air of being a confirmed old bachelor. It's a good front, but it doesn't fool me."

"Careful there, old bean. You're coming dangerously close to knowing all my secrets."

I smiled at him. "Only because I know the real you. The person behind the monocle and the walking stick and the perfectly turned-out evening kit. And I like the *you* underneath all the bachelor trappings. Believe me, when it comes to Vogel, there is no spark there at all. You have no reason to be jealous."

"I'm glad to hear it. Sorry to have been an idiot."

"No apology needed." I put my other hand over his.

"You know, I had my own bout with the green-eyed monster, as you called it, when it came to Miss Ravenna, so I shan't throw stones."

We smiled at each other, then became aware of a gaze leveled on us from one of the guests at a nearby table. "Perhaps we should discuss that sleigh ride . . . ?"

"Excellent idea, but I believe it's started snowing again," Jasper said.

"Only lightly, and there is no wind at all. With the snow, it would be all the more reason to snuggle together in the sleigh under some blankets."

"Sounds like an excellent way to end the evening." He caught the waiter's eye. "Check, please."

CHAPTER 25

*T*he next morning, I took my notebook with me when I went down to breakfast. I chose a table by the window, where the sun was streaming in, glittering on the tines of the fork and flashing off the blade of the knife. The snowstorm was over, and only a few thin clouds lingered on the mountains, but they were drifting away from the valley, slowly retreating over the rocky peaks like the train of an evening gown disappearing as a woman walked up a staircase. A fresh layer of brilliant white coated the village.

While I waited for my food, I sipped my tea and began to make notes. Since Mrs. Lavington's death, I'd been jotting down my thoughts. I detailed what I'd learned yesterday about Etta and Fredrick as well as what Juliet had told me about the blackmail notes, then added Mr. Tobinn to my list with a question mark by his name.

I moved the pen along the names: Hattie, Rob, Mr. Lavington, Mrs. Ashford, Etta Morgan, and Mr. Tobinn. I wanted to cross off Mrs. Ashford and Etta. Based on their

SARA ROSETT

personalities alone, I didn't think either one of them would murder Mrs. Lavington, but I didn't have any real proof they hadn't done it, so they had to stay on the list. I categorized them as *unlikely due to personality*.

I could picture Hattie with her quick temper lashing out. She went into the category of *definitely possible*. Rob and Mr. Lavington went into my *possible but murky* category. I couldn't eliminate them, and I didn't have much information to go on about either one of them. Mr. Lavington was still mostly keeping to his room, which made it difficult to pin him down for a conversation. Hattie was guarding Rob like a terrier, keeping our paths from crossing, so I'd had no luck talking with him again.

A shadow fell across the table. "May I join you?" Jasper asked.

"Please do."

He asked for a cup of coffee, and I requested a fresh pot of tea. Jasper inched his chair around so that the sun wasn't full on his face. "I must say I quite enjoyed the sleigh ride. One of your best ideas, old bean."

"I agree." With the tiny flakes falling it had felt as if we were in a snow globe.

We grinned at each other until the waiter moved between us, breaking our eye contact.

"What will you do today?" Jasper asked.

"A bit of shopping this morning for souvenirs since we only have a few days left. I don't want to leave that until the last moment." I refilled my teacup. "You're up bright and early." Jasper was not an early bird, and I was surprised to see him at breakfast.

"As you said, we only have a few more days here, and I

want to make the most of it. I've finished the difficult bit of my project."

"Hooray," I said and lifted my teacup in a toast.

He mirrored my gesture with his coffee. "I only need to make a clean copy to hand off to Bebe. She and Mr. Vandenberg are returning today. Once I'm done with that, perhaps I can join you on your souvenir hunt. I must get Grigsby one of those snow globes that you described."

"Is that the sort of thing he'd like?" I'd only spoken to Jasper's valet on the telephone, but I pictured him as stiff and prissy. Basically a wet blanket. He had the rather stuffy belief that young ladies shouldn't telephone gentlemen and managed to convey his attitude through the telephone line. I couldn't imagine something as frivolous as a snow globe would appeal to him.

"It's not for him. It's for his niece."

"Oh. What a strange thought—Grigsby around children."

"He's quite fond of his sister's brood. He keeps me *au courant* on their doings. The older boys are away at school, but the youngest is still at home. Grigsby says she commands him to participate in her doll tea parties when he visits."

"What a mind-boggling thought."

Jasper glanced at my notebook. "What are you working on there?"

I shook off the curious image of a valet at a doll tea party. "It's a list of people connected with Mrs. Lavington. But I'm not making much headway in figuring out what truly happened."

Jasper put down his coffee. "May I?"

"Please. You're as fond of puzzles as I am." I turned the notebook toward him.

He read over it and tapped the last name on the page. "Who is this Mr. Galen V. Tobinn?"

"He reserved the middle room on the top floor at the back of the hotel but didn't arrive. He canceled later. It's important because of the icicles. Someone needed access to the room to knock them down."

"Ah, yes. To set the scene. So access to that room, and that balcony, were important for the staging of the crime."

"Exactly. Mr. Tobinn booked the room about a week before. Vogel has inquiries out with Cook's for more details."

Jasper made a humming sound as he tapped the last name. "Tobinn with two *n*s. Bit unusual, the double *n*."

"Perhaps it's German, like Bonn."

"Yes," Jasper said, but he drew out the word as if he were testing the idea. Our breakfast arrived, and I closed the notebook. Shortly afterward, Miss Ravenna and Mr. Vandenberg swept in and joined us.

"How was the tour of the Lower Engadine Valley?" I asked after they turned in their breakfast order.

"Absolutely wonderful." Miss Ravenna extended her left hand, fingers angled down. A large diamond glittered on her ring finger.

"Oh, congratulations," I said, and Jasper added well wishes as well. Mr. Vandenberg sat back in his chair, a contented look on his face as he gazed at Miss Ravenna.

"You must tell us all about it," I said.

"Evert proposed in the most splendid setting. We were on a balcony with the Alps spread out around us, and it was . . . absolutely perfect." Miss Ravenna tilted her head down and sent Mr. Vandenberg a coy glance.

"One must set the scene, no?" he said lightly.

"That's what happens when a director proposes," Miss Ravenna said, still flirting with her eyes as she sipped her coffee.

"When is the wedding?" I asked Miss Ravenna.

"Sometime in the summer."

Mr. Vandenberg added, "You're both invited, of course. We have yet to decide where the ceremony will take place."

Miss Ravenna waved her hand. "Details, details. We'll work all that out later. For now, we are a giddy engaged couple."

Their breakfast arrived, and as our conversation turned to what they planned to do during their last days in St. Moritz, Mr. Lavington passed by our table. He was clean-shaven, and his jumper and trousers were immaculate, but he still had a haggard air about him. His face seemed thinner, which made his strong jaw seem even more prominent. He gave us a short nod as he followed the maître d' to an unoccupied table in the corner of the room. He took a seat with his back to the room.

Once he was out of earshot, a more subdued expression replaced the glowing, smitten look on Miss Ravenna's face. "I'm surprised the poor man is still here."

I said, "He's mostly been holed up in his room since his wife died."

Miss Ravenna cocked her head to the side questioningly. "I would have thought he'd have returned to England for the funeral."

"The body hasn't been released," I said.

"Really? Do the authorities think it wasn't an accident?"

"That's what Korporale Vogel is trying to determine."

Jasper added, "With Olive's help."

When Vogel arrived at the chalet and found me talking with Juliet, he hadn't actually welcomed me back to the investigation, but I didn't want to get into my murky status at the moment.

Miss Ravenna nodded. "I can see why he would enlist you. You're here in the hotel, and you're from the same social set as Mrs. Lavington. Have you made any progress?"

"I've uncovered a few interesting facts, but nothing specifically answers the question of whether or not Mrs. Lavington's death was an accident."

"I see. Well, I wish you the best of luck, and I'm thrilled that I'm not on the suspect list this time."

Mr. Vandenberg turned to her with a frown, and Miss Ravenna said, "Oh, haven't I told you about that, darling? It happened at Christmas . . ."

The rest of breakfast was spent recounting the incident at Holly Hill Lodge. As we made our way out of the restaurant, Jasper said to Miss Ravenna, "I'll be doing some typing this morning. The project I was working on is complete. I only need to make a clear copy."

"That's wonderful news."

Jasper went off to consult with the manager about borrowing their typewriter, and I went up to my room to put away my notebook. Quick footsteps sounded on the stairs behind me, then Etta fell into step with me. "Miss Belgrave, I'm glad I caught you. I'm leaving the hotel this afternoon to go to the valley where Fredrick's family lives.

If you have a moment, would you mind coming along to my room? I have something I'd like to give you."

"Have you found another remnant of a note?"

She let out a little laugh. "No, nothing like that. I have a gift for you to thank you for your help."

"You didn't have to do that."

"I wanted to. If this isn't a convenient time, I can leave it with the front desk."

"No, now is fine." I dropped off my notebook in my room, then went down the hall to her room, where she she'd just unlocked her door. I followed her in. She handed me a small tissue-wrapped package. "I know I put you in a rather awkward position, asking you to speak to the police on my behalf, and I do appreciate your help. It's a little something that I made."

I opened the package. A maroon-colored scarf rested in the tissue. The material was familiar. Where had I seen it? Perhaps in a shop window? "It's beautiful. Thank you." I shook it out to admire it, tracing my hand over the silky material. It would be perfect to wear around my throat tied with a square knot. "It will look lovely with my rather plain coat. And it's the same shade as your blouse," I added.

"Yes, I made them both."

"Did you? You're an excellent seamstress." I could sew, but the tiny, perfectly spaced stitches on the edge of the scarf showed that her skill with a needle went far beyond mine.

"I had time on my hands, and I certainly don't like to see anything go to waste."

"What do you mean?"

She looked away, suddenly flustered, then wrinkled

her nose. "I hope you won't think it shoddy of me, but I salvaged the material from a dress that had been thrown away." Before I could assure her that didn't bother me, she rushed on. "Mrs. Lavington often gave me her clothes at the end of the season, and I'd remake them into a different style, something more appropriate for my station. I did that with the dress that Fredrick found in the rubbish." Her face softened. "He remembered that I liked to sew, and how I like to remake things from castoffs."

"This is from the dress Juliet wore on the evening of the fire, isn't it?" I asked as the memory clicked into place.

"Yes. She'd thrown it out," Etta said, disapproval lacing her words. "The cuff of the sleeve was charred, but the bodice and the skirt were perfectly fine. When one is in my situation, one must be thrifty," she added, her tone becoming apologetic. "If you don't want it, I completely understand."

"Oh no. It's beautiful, and I have to be frugal myself. If it weren't for my cousin's castoffs, my wardrobe would be sparse." Her blouse wasn't a simple pattern. The full sleeves and pin tucks elevated it beyond a basic design. "You must have had quite a lot of material to work with."

"The burnt part of the sleeve had to go, of course, and I couldn't do much with the rest of the tulle, but"—she waved a hand in a motion that encompassed both her blouse and the scarf—"the silk that made up the bodice and the velvet skirt were fine. I made sure the fabric didn't smell of smoke. I left it on my balcony overnight to air, and it was fine the next morning. Such a shame about the underdress, though. I couldn't do a thing with it, although I did try. It was too stiff. In the end, I had to throw it out." She glanced toward the rubbish bin, which was full of a pale pink material.

"How odd. I've never seen anything like that used in a lady's evening gown." The room was so small that the rubbish bin was only a step away. I ran my hand over the material. It was a dense weave, thick and stiff.

"Neither have I. I thought it was used to give structure to the dress since this silk drapes in such a flowy manner. Or perhaps it was for warmth. It is February in the Alps."

"I suppose that could be the case, but it's so rough and stiff. It wouldn't be comfortable against one's skin."

"I agree. That's why I discarded it in the end. Someone could probably come up with a use for it, but I couldn't think of anything." She pulled the pieces of the thick fabric out of the rubbish. "You're welcome to it, if you'd like to give it a go. See, here's the sleeve. It's from the side that wasn't burnt, of course. That piece you're holding was part of the bodice. And this was the skirt." She unfolded the largest piece of cloth. The material had printing on it. The letters *AS* covered the whole section of the fabric. The stem of another letter was visible next to the *S*, but the rest of the word had been cut away. A memory stirred of a similar fabric with printing on it. It was such a momentous thought that I caught my breath.

"Miss Belgrave? Are you all right?"

I came out of my reverie. "Yes, fine. Thank you. You said the whole dress had this fabric underneath?"

"Yes, an underdress, or a sort of stiff lining, you might say."

I examined the front and back of the rest of the fabric Etta had pulled out of the rubbish, but none of the other pieces had letters printed on them. "I will take this, thank you," I said, bundling it together.

"Here, you can wrap it in this, if you'd like." She took out several layers of tissue paper.

We folded it into a bulky packet with the tissue around it, then I folded the scarf on top of it. With the package tucked under my arm, I crossed to the door. "Thank you again for the beautiful scarf, and best wishes for you in your new life."

After Etta had said goodbye and closed the door, I went downstairs, out the door, and across the bridge to the sun terrace. The sun was higher in the sky now, and with the shelter of the building blocking the wind, it was pleasantly warm. Mr. Vandenberg and Miss Ravenna were standing at the far end, leaning on the wooden railing, admiring the mountain view. I rushed over. "I'm so sorry to interrupt, but may I ask you a question?"

"Yes, of course," Miss Ravenna said.

I tucked the scarf into my skirt pocket, put the bundle down on a nearby chaise, and pushed back the tissue. "Do you know what sort of fabric this is?"

Miss Ravenna ran her hand across it. "My, it's thick. Some sort of canvas?"

"Mr. Vandenberg?" I asked. "Is there anything familiar about it?" I found the section with the printed letters on it and held it up.

He took a step back, tipped his head to one side, and then his face cleared. "It's a piece of a safety curtain, I believe."

Miss Ravenna said, "A fire curtain? Oh yes, I can see it now."

CHAPTER 26

I sat down with a plop on another chaise lounge as Miss Ravenna reached for the fabric. "I didn't recognize it with it all chopped up. What would you want with a fire curtain, Olive?"

"It's not what *I* want with a fire curtain, but what would *Juliet* want with one?"

"I'm afraid you've lost me," Miss Ravenna said.

"I'll explain later. Right now I need to know more about this fabric. It's asbestos, correct? You're both theater people. You must be familiar with it."

Miss Ravenna darted a glance at Mr. Vandenberg, then said to me, "Perhaps you have a touch of altitude sickness? A glass of water and a little rest out of the sun will help."

"It's kind of you to be concerned, but I'm fine. I don't have altitude sickness, and I promise I haven't taken leave of my senses. I need to know about the fabric for the investigation."

Miss Ravenna's face cleared. "Oh, in that case, I won't

be much help. I don't know much about safety curtains, only that they're to prevent fires from spreading, if one is unlucky enough to be on stage when there's an accident. Evert, perhaps you know more?"

"Not much more than you've said, darling." He'd picked up the piece with the letters and now handed it back to me. "There were some horrible tragedies before they were developed. This looks to be quite old and worn. I imagine this was probably thrown out when a replacement curtain was put up. That happened a few years ago in a theater in Munich where I was directing a play."

"So the fabric itself is fireproof?" I asked.

"I'm by no means an expert, but I believe it is," Mr. Vandenberg said. "It's fire-retardant, at a minimum."

I thanked them, then rewrapped the bundle and went inside. I didn't want to wait for the lift, so I dashed up the stairs to my room. I shrugged into my coat, crammed my hat on my head, and picked up the tissue-wrapped fabric. As I stepped into the hallway and pulled my door closed, Jasper trotted up the stairs.

"There you are, old bean. I've been trying to run you to ground. I have something that might be of interest to you."

"I can't stop. I'm on my way to see Vogel."

"Perfect timing, then." He held out a sheet of paper with the name Galen V. Tobinn typed across the top with a space between each letter. "I couldn't get this name out of my mind, so I fiddled around with the letters."

Underneath the typewritten letters, Jasper's neat handwriting marched down the page in a list of what looked like nonsense. He'd rearranged the letters into various combinations. He pointed to the last line.

"Ben Lavington?" I said. "Galen V. Tobinn is an anagram?" I was gobsmacked. "Are you sure?" I asked automatically, but then immediately I said, "Of course you are. Oh my."

The fabric bundle began to slip. Jasper said, "Here, let me," and took it from me.

"You think Mr. Lavington reserved the middle room." I folded the paper with the anagram into fourths and slipped it in my coat pocket.

"It's certainly a possibility that Vogel should be made aware of."

Several isolated incidents—little memories—bubbled to the surface and blended together, creating a picture that I hadn't seen until that moment. I leaned against the wall. "It certainly is." I spoke more to myself than to Jasper as I realized what had happened. "Oh my," I repeated. "I don't know why I didn't see it before. The fire—and Mrs. Lavington's death—oh, this means they coordinated everything between them." It was as if a fog were burning off, and I could see the horizon clearly.

Jasper asked. "Mr. Lavington and who?"

I poked the paper-wrapped bundle he held. "Juliet." I described the material and how Etta had come to have it. "The fabric is fireproof, or at least fire resistant. Juliet *planned* to set her dress on fire. It was a distraction."

Jasper looked from the bundle to me, his brows lowered as an expression of incredulity passed across his face. Then the enormity of what I was saying hit him. "But that's . . . mad."

"Absolutely bonkers, yes. But with the fabric, she'd be protected from a burn. Mr. Lavington left immediately to get help." I felt my shoulders drop as I looked up to the ceiling, shaking my head at myself. "I should have seen it! How did I miss it?

"Seen what, Olive?"

"Yesterday, when I went to the chalet with Juliet, her necklace caught on her scarf and fell to the floor. I picked up the necklace and gave it back to her. It had a medallion on it, a solid gold piece with a design engraved on it, the letter *J* with some embellishments, a leafy vine. But the vine wasn't just decoration, it was the letter *B*." I closed my eyes, frustrated at myself. "A vine with two loops on the side of the *J*. It was subtle, and I missed it when I glanced at it, but now that I know . . ." I flapped my hand at the bundle of fabric. "It's so very obvious. It was their initials, *J* for Juliet and *B* for Ben Lavington, linked together."

I spun away and paced up the corridor, nearly mowing down a stubby man who'd come out of his room. He reared back and skirted around me before pacing quickly away.

"I've been *such* an idiot." I reached the end of the hall and paced back. "How could I have not seen it? They must have conspired together to set up the whole thing. Juliet used the blackmail payment to lure Mrs. Lavington to the terrace, and Mr. Lavington left the lounge, not to get a doctor, but to," I swallowed, "kill her. It must have been Juliet and Mr. Lavington who I overheard on the train, planning Mrs. Lavington's death."

I resumed my trek down the hall but walked slowly. "But how did Mr. Lavington get onto the terrace without leaving footprints?"

As I turned back to him, Jasper switched the package

from one arm to the other. "When I went up with Mr. Hoffman to tell him about his wife, he seemed so stunned. I had the manager bring up a brandy, and once he'd had that, he became a veritable font of words, even if they were jumbled. He said he'd asked where the nearest doctor lived when he left the lounge and had run all the way there and back. Now that I think about it, it would have made more sense for him to have asked at the front desk if the doctor was on the telephone line—they often are now."

"But in our agitated state—with the scare of the fire—none of us even questioned his plan."

"He put it in motion so quickly that there wasn't time. That must have been intentional. In the heat of the moment, people make decisions that later seem quite illogical."

"And now we know that even if Mr. Vandenberg hadn't snatched up the hearthrug and snuffed out the flames, Juliet wouldn't have been seriously injured," I said with a pointed look at the bundle of fabric. "So no one saw Mr. Lavington from the time he left the hotel until he returned later, looking quite disheveled, if I remember correctly."

"Yes, Grigsby would have disapproved. Besides being rumpled, his suit jacket was torn at the shoulder seam. I noticed that when we were having a drink afterward."

I halted by Jasper, working through the possible variations on Mr. Lavington's story. "Yes, I noticed it as well. He or Juliet must have known the correct address for the doctor and that number seven was unoccupied. He might not have even gone to that lane at all. No one saw him there. What if he went directly to the terrace?" I rubbed my temple. "But how did he get to Mrs. Lavington without reentering the hotel and going across the bridge to the terrace or going across the snow on the ground around the terrace? That's still the question."

CHAPTER 27

"There's only one thing to do, old bean," Jasper said, his tone incredibly practical. "Let's go down and have a look. Perhaps this new information will spark fresh possibilities."

Since I had no other ideas, I agreed. We went down the stairs, out the door, and over the little bridge to the terrace. Miss Ravenna and Mr. Vandenberg were no longer there. Another couple sat on the chaise lounges at the far end closest to the mountain. I walked to the side nearest the hotel. I dragged one of the chaise lounges roughly into the position it had been in that night. "This is where Mrs. Lavington was found, lying on the decking beside the chair."

"Was there anything else around her?"

"Just one of these little tables." I pulled the nearest one over and brushed the snow from the top of it with a few swipes of my bare hand. I shook off the moisture and blotted my palm against my skirt. The sun was warm, but the snow was still icy cold. I stopped mid-movement and stared at the dark wooden tabletop. "Of course!"

I stepped to the railing of the balustrade and dusted snow away. My fingers were freezing, but I hardly noticed. Jasper joined me. "Had a thought?"

"I'll say. Jasper, you're brilliant!"

I dashed over to the side of the terrace where the ground dropped away and leaned over to have a look at the rocks that formed the retaining wall. "You were exactly right," I called to Jasper, who was ambling toward me.

He reached my side and peered over. "While I'm delighted with your assessment, and you have obviously seen the proverbial light, I'm still quite in the dark. Midnight black over here, actually. You're thinking Mr. Lavington could climb up this way, I believe."

"Yes, that's right."

Jasper set the bundle of fabric on one of the chaise lounges, then, hands in his pockets, leaned over the railing to study the drop again. "It's sheer, but I imagine Mr. Lavington could navigate it quite easily, especially if he had an ice axe or something of the sort, even in evening kit. Of course, formal wear isn't made for vigorous climbing, which could explain the tear in his jacket." He turned, hands still in his pockets, and studied the distance to the chaise. "But you said there were no tracks in the snow on the terrace. It's rather a long distance to where Mrs. Lavington was."

"But if he walked on the railing he could get to her and leave the snow on the terrace pristine." I motioned to the railing that ran along the back of the terrace. "If he climbed up on the railing here," I patted the diagonal cut where the two boards of the railing joined at the corner, "he could walk straight down to her. It wouldn't be hard for a mountaineer to walk along a board a few inches wide. Wouldn't he navigate small ridges and narrow paths all the time? A flat board would be mundane stuff for him."

Jasper eyed the railing and the chaise. "Yes, I can see how he could pull that off."

The couple at the other end of the terrace returned to the hotel. I watched them leave, but my thoughts were still on what had happened that snowy night. "So Mr. Lavington ran out of the hotel, came around here, and climbed up the wall, most likely using an ice axe to help him gain purchase. He must have hidden it somewhere nearby. Then all he had to do was walk along the railing to reach his wife."

Jasper shaded his eyes as he looked across the terrace to the bridge that connected it to the hotel. "You think he —what?—dusted the snow off of the whole length of the railing—all the way to the bridge—and hoped that no one would notice the discrepancy of the snow-free railing and the snow-covered terrace?"

"Yes, I think that's what he *must* have done. He could have swept it away with his feet." I described the overhead photo Vogel had shown me. "The railing next to the hotel was dark in the photos taken from above, but when I looked at the terrace from ground-level, I didn't even notice it. I was so focused on the chaise, the footprints, and the snow on the terrace and the surrounding ground that it didn't even register that one side of the terrace's railings wasn't covered in snow. And then later, no one noticed it either, even in the photos."

Jasper tipped his head back, wrinkles cutting into the corners of his eyes as he squinted. "And even if someone had noticed it, the lack of snow on the railing might have been written off. The eaves might have protected the back edge of the terrace, depending on if there was a wind. I can see how it could be overlooked." Jasper shifted his attention back to the lone chaise lounge near the back railing. "You said there was no sign of a struggle?"

"No."

"Then why would Mrs. Lavington sit there, watch her husband approach in such an unorthodox way, and then let him conk her on the head?"

"She said she was exhausted, remember? Did you see how she was yawning? No, that's right, your back was to her. I was sleepy myself, and even I noticed it. Bad manners to yawn, even if you're not acclimated to the altitude. I wonder if Mr. Lavington slipped something into her drink to make her woozy? They did have drinks at the card table. It would have been easy for him to do it, especially if he fetched a round of drinks as Rob did when we were there. I wonder if there was an autopsy? Surely that would show if she'd been drugged. Korporale Vogel didn't mention one, so I'm not sure they did one."

Jasper had shifted to look back down the drop to the lane. "And then . . . afterward, Mr. Lavington must have climbed down the wall and returned the ice axe to wherever he had hidden it before returning to the hotel."

We both fell silent. I was contemplating the awful cold-bloodedness of the whole scenario. If we were right, it had been carefully planned. The thought of working out so many minute details with such a goal turned my stomach.

Jasper, head bent, hands in his pockets as he studied the sheer wall, said, "An ice axe would make an excellent weapon."

A shiver of revulsion coursed through me. "Yes, as terrible as that thought is, it's true. And I suppose the type of wound it would leave could be mistaken for an icicle falling from a considerable height."

We both tilted our heads back and looked at the crystal spikes that hung from the eaves, dripping in the sunlight. I said, "He could have knocked off the icicles later, after we all went upstairs. In fact, he could have done it before he came to my door looking for Mrs. Lavington." Arms crossed and lost in thought, I said, "That's a lot of activity. Would there be enough time to do it?"

"It depends on how long we were occupied in the lounge. It took at least five to ten minutes to put out the fire and calm Juliet. And we also had to extinguish the smoldering furniture she bumped against."

"And then Mr. Hoffman came. It had to have been at least a quarter hour, if not longer, before we came out into the lobby and saw Mr. Lavington return," I said.

"I agree," Jasper said. "I imagine that's enough time to get to the terrace and back. Mrs. Lavington's absence wasn't noticed until quite a while after the fire."

"And it was Mr. Lavington who drew attention to the fact that she was missing. He wouldn't have done that until he'd set the stage with the icicles. Between the time the fire in the lounge was put out and when Mrs. Lavington's body was discovered, Mr. Lavington would have had time to go to Mr. Tobinn's unoccupied room on the top floor. Vogel says the locks on the doors here aren't that secure."

"One of his wife's hairpins would do the trick," Jasper agreed. "And then, careful not to disturb the snow on the balcony railing, he swatted at the icicles with the broom until some fell onto the terrace."

I turned away from the railing and went across to the chaise. "I really *must* find Vogel," I said as I picked up the bundle of fabric.

Jasper took it from me. "I'll come along."

A few moments later, we were crossing the lobby when I spotted Vogel at the front desk. I touched Jasper's arm, and we changed course.

"Well met, Miss Belgrave," Vogel said. "I have some news you might be interested in, but I can't speak to you at the moment."

"I have news for you as well," I said. "It's terribly important."

"How intriguing." He moved away, speaking over his shoulder as he followed Mr. Hoffman across the lobby. "I'll be with you in shortly."

"But it is urgent. *Quite* urgent." I quickened my steps and caught up with him. "Mr. Lavington and Juliet worked together to kill Mrs. Lavington. I know it sounds—"

"I agree wholeheartedly."

"—rather fantastical, but—wait." I was so stunned I stopped walking. Vogel and Mr. Hoffman hadn't halted. I scurried to catch up with them near the lift. "What did you say?"

"I've reached the same conclusion," Vogel said. "I'm on my way to visit Mr. Lavington." Jasper was also keeping pace with the group, and Vogel noticed the bundle Jasper held. "It looks like you have something for me?"

"Yes, evidence."

Mr. Hoffman pushed the button for the lift, and it trundled downward. "Excellent," Vogel said. "I think, Miss Belgrave, that we didn't part on the best of terms. At least you were not happy with my suggestion you return to your holiday."

"No, I couldn't. I'm a see-it-through type of girl."

Vogel's eyebrows flared, and he murmured, "See-it-through," as if filing the expression away for use later. "You're persistent, yes."

Jasper made a strange sound halfway between a choke and a snort. I leveled a look at him.

"Oh, come now, Olive," Jasper said, "I know better than anyone you don't give up."

The lift had arrived and Mr. Hoffman pushed the grate back. "An admirable quality," Vogel agreed. "I apologize if I, um, cut you off at the pass, Miss Belgrave." He grinned at his metaphor. I closed my eyes and gave a little huffing laugh. "I'm glad that we are friends again." He motioned to the parcel. "And I look forward to hearing about your latest discovery, but please forgive me. I must see Mr. Lavington immediately." He entered the lift, where Mr. Hoffman was waiting, a ring of keys in hand.

As the lift crawled upward, I said to Jasper, "Let's have a seat over here," and we went to a pair of armchairs set against the wall with a view of the lift. We'd just sat down when Juliet burst into the lobby, brushing past the new doorman. She wore outdoor clothing—a thick jumper, tweed knee-length breeches, and leather nailed boots, which clicked across the herringbone parquet as she strode to the front desk. She didn't have a hat, and her hair was disheveled, some of it standing out from her head with static electricity. Little clumps of snow clung to her clothing, and the skin of her nose and cheekbones was pink, as if she'd been in the mountain sunshine for too long.

She'd jerked off her gloves as she walked, then leaned over the desk as she spoke to the attendant, her voice tense and her words carrying. "I need to speak to Korporale Vogel. I was informed that he's here. Find him at once."

The tissue wrapped around the bundle of fabric was gaping, and the weave of the fabric was visible. The paper crinkled as I squashed it back into place. Jasper adjusted his hold, clamping down on the unruly section of the parcel.

I couldn't hear the attendant's soothing murmur of an answer as he looked toward the lift. Juliet turned on her heel and made her way across the lobby. The lift had begun its creaking descent, and I expected it to be empty, but Mr. Hoffman pulled back the grate, and Vogel stepped out.

Juliet practically pounced on him. "Korporale, thank goodness I found you."

"Good afternoon, Miss Lenox. How may I assist you?"

She gulped. "It's horrible. Absolutely the most vile thing!"

"Please, miss, calm yourself."

People walking through the lobby slowed to stare, but Juliet was oblivious. Her words were choppy as she gulped in a shuddering breath. "Mr. Lavington attacked me."

CHAPTER 28

*V*ogel's expression of polite concern remained unchanged for a few seconds as Juliet's eyes watered. Gulps and little hiccup-like sobs punctured her words as she said, "I was . . . skiing . . ."

Vogel looked at Mr. Hoffman. "Perhaps we might use the lounge privately?"

"Of course, Korporale. I'll see to it that you're not disturbed." He was already ushering Vogel and Juliet to the lounge.

Over Juliet's hunched shoulders, Vogel looked at Jasper and me and jerked his head, indicating that we should follow him.

The lounge was empty, and Mr. Hoffman steered Juliet to one of the club chairs grouped around a table near the bar, then gave Vogel a nod and left, closing the door.

Jasper and I lingered by the door. Vogel joined us and pitched his voice low enough that only Jasper and I could hear. "Mr. Lavington's not in his room. The doorman said he didn't leave the hotel this morning by the front doors, so he must have slipped out through the exit in the kitchen." He looked at Juliet, seated across the room. "It seems we are participants in a little drama. I assume I can count on you to participate in this parlor game?"

Jasper, who was always amiable said, "Of course. And I'm sure Olive is in as well. She's a good egg when it comes to games. Charades, murder parties, scavenger hunts. We've done them all, haven't we, old bean?"

Vogel blinked at Jasper's words. I was sure his attention had snagged on *murder party*, but instead of explaining, I asked, "What do you want us to do?"

"Simply play along. Follow me, please." He raised his voice to a normal level as he made his way through the tables. "Miss Belgrave is here, Miss Lenox. I thought you'd like a lady here to support you."

"And here I am without my smelling salts," I said sotto voce to Jasper, then added in a normal tone, "Perhaps a glass of water?" I went to the bar and found a tumbler while Jasper tucked the paper-wrapped parcel of fabric into one of the club chairs at another table and turned it away from Juliet, hiding it from her view. Vogel handed Juliet his handkerchief. She dabbed at her eyes, wiped her nose, and took a sip from the glass I'd set in front of her.

Vogel indicated I should take the chair beside Juliet. The door hinges squeaked, and Mr. Hoffman stepped partially into the room. He held up a folded piece of paper. Vogel went to meet him and read the note. They had a short low-voiced discussion, then the manager left, and Vogel returned to our group.

Juliet set the glass down. "I'm sorry. It was just so, so frightening." Her eyes were red-rimmed and her lashes stuck together in little wet spikes. In addition to being pink, the tip of her nose was now shiny.

"Yes, I can see you're distraught." Vogel sat down across the table. "Let's start at the beginning, Miss Lenox. You were skiing?"

"Um—yes." She balled the handkerchief into her palm and pushed her hair back from her face. "After the storm, there was a gorgeous layer of fresh snow."

"Good. Good," Vogel said. "And were you alone or with someone else?"

Juliet shot a quick look at Jasper, who'd taken a seat at the next table near the paper-wrapped bundle. He sat with one knee crossed over the other. He'd put his monocle on and was examining his fingernails.

Vogel said, "Miss Belgrave and Mr. Rimington need to speak to me, but I believe your news is most urgent. Now, you were skiing, yes?"

"That's right. I went out alone. I went to the slope above the Immergrün Valley. Do you know it?"

Vogel stared at her for a second, then leaned forward, a concerned look on his face. "I do, but that is quite a tricky area. The drop-off —"

"Only if you go near the edge, which I never do." She swiped her hand back and forth over the center of the table. "I only swish back and forth across the open area in the center of the slope. It was just me and the sky and the snow. So lovely." She dropped her gaze to her lap as she folded the handkerchief into a square. "I saw another skier out of the corner of my eye. Usually, everyone keeps well away from each other, especially there, and I didn't think anything of it."

She sniffed and swallowed, her attention fixed on

creasing the fabric into a smaller square. "It was Ben—Mr. Lavington. I recognized him from his jacket and his hat— bright blue, like his eyes." She tilted her head just enough that she could shoot a quick glance at Vogel. "I saw him coming my way, and I raised my hand in greeting." She mimed the motion, lifting her closed fist as if she held a ski pole. "But instead of keeping his distance, as people usually do, he came right at me, forcing me to the edge." She swept her hand across to the edge of the table to illustrate. "I was so shocked. I barely had time to react."

"And what did you do?" Vogel had taken his notebook and pen from his pocket and was writing.

"I didn't know what had happened, if he was playing at some mad game . . . or . . . what." She gulped, pressed the fabric to her nose for a moment, then pulled it away and said in a rush, "To avoid him, I skied nearer the edge. I'd never been that close. I could even see the drop to the valley far below. It was the most frightening thing I've ever seen. I tucked in and gained enough speed to get slightly ahead of him, then I leaned into a turn, which took me away from the edge. I cut right across in front of him. We were so close I nearly ran over his skis. I could have touched him." She drew a deep breath, and her shoulders dropped. "And then I was away, shooting across the snow toward the trees, thank goodness. He tried to turn too, but he was going too fast. He sailed right off the edge." She made a downward curving motion with her hand. "And then there was the most horrible crashing, crunching sound." She dropped her voice to a whisper. "And it's all because I know what happened—what he did to Emmaline."

"And what was that?" Vogel asked.

She twisted the handkerchief around. Her words barely audible, she said, "He murdered her."

Vogel didn't react, and I took my cue from him and didn't try to manufacture a surprised look. Jasper was now tugging at a thread on his sleeve.

Juliet looked up, her brows pressed together, her gaze racing from Vogel to me. She licked her lips. "You don't seem surprised."

Vogel shook his head. "I'm not. I suspected—Miss Belgrave also—we both suspected Mrs. Lavington's death was murder."

"Oh." Juliet glanced at me and seemed to shrink into the chair away from me. "Oh. But you said you weren't investigating. I thought—"

Vogel asked, "What happened between you and Mr. Lavington? You were lovers?"

She hesitated but then seemed to decide denying it wouldn't help her. "Well, yes. He and I began a liaison a few months back, and he convinced me . . . to help him. He said it was a little prank. I didn't realize Ben would use me in the way he did."

"In what way was that, Miss Lenox?" Vogel asked, pen poised over his notebook, his face expectant, but not sympathetic.

"You're aware of the little joke I played on Emmaline with the notes and the money, which were very small sums of cash, you must agree. I've explained all that. It was a bit of fun, that's all, but Ben used me. I had no idea he was manipulating me to make sure his wife was on the terrace that night. That's as far as my involvement went in her death. Ben did it. He killed her. He's to blame, not me."

Vogel asked, "So you asked Mrs. Lavington to bring the money to the terrace?"

"Yes, you already know all this. I told you that yesterday. I sent the note to her to be on the terrace at ten, but my sleeve caught fire. In all the chaos, meeting her completely went out of my head." Juliet dabbed at her eyes again. "I had no idea Ben would use my—er—appointment with Emmaline as an opportunity to do away with her."

"Terrible. Yes, a terrible story." Vogel put an emphasis on the word *story* as he set his pen down. "But I do not think it is the truth."

CHAPTER 29

*J*uliet, handkerchief pressed to the corner of one of her eyes, was drawing deep, shuddering breaths, which I thought was a precursor to a crescendo of sobs, but she looked up, blinking her spiky eyelashes. "What?"

"I believe you're lying," Vogel enunciated each word and then sat back, arms crossed.

She went still and stared at him a moment, her chest rising and falling, reminding me of a newsreel I'd seen once of a tiger preparing to stalk its prey. "I don't know what you mean," she finally said, her voice going softer and her expression shifting to a combination of a hurt and perplexed look. "Obviously, I was horrified—*terrifically* horrified—at what happened. It was vile! He took advantage of the fire to slip out and kill Emmaline. Once I figured out what had happened, I tried to convince him to turn himself in, but he threatened me. He said he'd kill me if I said anything about it. I had *nothing* to do with it, I promise. It was all Ben."

Vogel said, "Quick thinking on his part."

"It was!" Juliet agreed, leaning toward him. "Ben was extremely devious. I had no idea what I was involved in."

"How did he do it?" Vogel asked, a shade of doubt in his voice. "Do you know?"

"Well, yes. He bragged about it—later." She blew her nose and straightened her spine. "Ben said he ran out of the hotel, scrambled up the wall on the side of the terrace. Once he'd scaled the wall, he walked along the railing. Since the snow had stopped, he had to do that so he wouldn't leave another set of footprints. He'd put one of Emmaline's sleeping powders in the last drink he brought to the table while they were playing cards. She didn't know a thing. She was out cold when he—um—struck her."

"And what did he hit her with?"

Juliet spread her hands, the wrinkled fabric of the handkerchief gripped in one palm with her thumb. "I don't know. I just know that Ben injured her and then managed to get back to the hotel before anyone saw him."

"And what if one of the guests at the back of the hotel had looked out their window?"

She shrugged. "He must have thought it would be unlikely. It was late. The drapes would be closed. It was a chance he took. He could be like that, a bit reckless. But it was always a calculated risk."

Vogel looked away as he pursed his lips together. "I come back to the point that it's quite an elaborate plan to conceive on the spur of the moment."

Under the table, Juliet's heel jiggled, a nervous moment that sent little tremors through the loose fabric of the breeches around her thighs. "Yes, but you don't understand what sort of man Ben was. He was polished and urbane, but underneath he was vicious and grasping."

"You had no knowledge of this plan?"

Juliet drew back as if the very idea were repulsive. "None. None at all. I'll admit I wasn't quite truthful a moment ago when I told you what happened on the mountain. In reality, the moment I saw him I was terrified. I don't think you understand what happened today. He tried to *kill* me." She braced an elbow on the arm of the chair and leaned over to massage the temple of her forehead.

"Has a rescue party gone out for Mr. Lavington?" Vogel asked.

Her head jerked up. "What? No. Why?" She glanced from Vogel to me, then amended her sharp tone to something more subdued. "I mean, it would be incredibly risky. Ben couldn't have survived that fall. I wouldn't want to endanger anyone else."

"Mountain rescues happen frequently. The climbers here are skilled." Vogel closed his notebook and tucked his pen away. "I will set that in motion, but first I believe Miss Belgrave has a point to add to our discussion." His glance flickered to the chair where Jasper had stowed the paper-wrapped bundle.

Ah, my turn to come on stage. "Yes, it's something I ran across today, something that was salvaged from the rubbish." I looked to Jasper. He dropped his monocle from his eye. The tissue whispered and crinkled as he picked it up.

"Put it just here, I think." I indicated the table in front of Juliet.

I peeled the thin paper back, exposing the fabric. Juliet

froze. "What is that?" Then her throat worked as she swallowed. "It's rather strange material, isn't it?" Her eyes were wide, and her expression opening and questioning, but her heel vibrated double-time.

"You don't know what this is?" I asked.

"No. I've no idea at all."

"That's strange because it came from the dress you wore on the night of the fire. It's a fireproof fabric, which rather throws doubt on your statements about knowing nothing of Mr. Lavington's plans to do away with his wife, wouldn't you say, Korporale?"

Korparale Vogel's eyebrows had gone skyward at my statement. Now he turned to Juliet as he said, "I quite agree, Miss Belgrave."

"A dress with a layer of material that doesn't burn . . . and a fire that drew everyone's attention to you. It begs the question, how could you not be part of the plan, Juliet? Perhaps you even designed it?"

She clamped her lips together and sat back in her chair.

Vogel reached for his pen. "Would you like to change anything about your statement, Miss Lenox?"

She pried her flattened lips apart and said, "I won't say another word unless I have a solicitor with me."

"I thought not. Very well." Vogel went to the door, and a moment later the stout older police officer followed Vogel into the room. Vogel said, "Swartz, escort Miss Lenox to the station. See she's settled in the cell before contacting her legal representative. Will handcuffs be necessary, Miss Lenox?"

Juliet eyed the door, then Swartz, with his pencil

mustache and broad shoulders. Still tight-lipped, she shook her head and shoved back her chair.

Vogel checked the clock on the wall, then said to the officer, "Quickly now. Take the exit in the kitchen. Oberwaller is waiting there for you with the motor." Swartz took Juliet's elbow in a firm grip and walked her out the door.

Vogel reached for the bundle of fabric, rewrapping it before tucking it under his arm. "I'm curious to hear the details on this, Miss Belgrave."

"Of course," I said as we walked with him to the lobby. "Juliet threw the dress away, and Miss Etta Morgan found it. Miss Morgan is the frugal type and decided to remake the silk into a blouse for her and a scarf for me. She'd discarded the underlayer, but I noticed it today when she gave me the scarf. One section of the fabric has printing on it. It took me a few moments to work out where I'd seen something similar. Once I hit on the thought that it might be a fire curtain, I confirmed my suspicions with Miss Bebe Ravenna and Mr. Evert Vandenberg."

Vogel paused by a large circular table near the hotel's doors. "They are two people who one could certainly rely on to identify a fire curtain. It is interesting that Miss Morgan should make you a scarf," Vogel murmured. "But I imagine that is of little importance."

I saw the little twinkle in his eye, and I inclined my head in agreement. "Trivial, actually, compared to the other things we've learned."

"Yes. I will need to confirm what you've told me with her, but that should be all the information I need from Miss Morgan."

"She'll be relieved to hear that."

Vogel looked to Jasper, who had watched the exchange, his gaze ping-ponging back and forth between us, and said, "You're lucky, Miss Belgrave, to have Mr. Rimington as your right-hand man. Did I get that expression right?"

"You are entirely correct in the word choice, and I couldn't agree more. In fact," I took the paper with the anagram from my pocket, "Jasper worked out that the full name of Mr. Tobinn is an anagram of Ben Lavington."

Vogel gave a little laugh as he took the paper. "Very perceptive. I hadn't worked that out. Although I heard back from my source at Cook's just an hour ago. The funds to cover the room came from a bank account owned by Benjamin Lavington. That detail was what convinced me to look deeper into Mr. Lavington's activities and motives."

"Do you believe Juliet's story about Mr. Lavington trying to send her into a crevasse?" I asked.

"I have serious doubts about it. That note Mr. Hoffman brought to me earlier was from one of my men with some related news." He glanced at his watch again, then looked out the window near the hotel's front doors. "Ah, right on time."

A small procession had halted outside. Mr. Hale and Mr. Blinkhorn held a stretcher between them with Mr. Lavington's body on it. Vogel went out to meet them. Jasper and I followed. For a moment, I wondered why they hadn't covered the body, but then Mr. Lavington turned his head and shouted, "Why are you stopping here, Blinkhorn? I need a doctor, not a hot bath."

Blinkhorn replied, "Instructions were to bring you here."

"What? Of all the blast—"

"Hello, Mr. Lavington." Vogel approached the stretcher. "The doctor is on his way here. He was called to one of the remote farms today. It will take him a while to return, which gives us time to chat. The hotel manager has put the lounge at my disposal. We'll make you comfortable there while we wait."

He motioned for the two men to carry the stretcher into the hotel. The doorman and Vogel held the doors wide, and Blinkhorn and Hale carefully climbed the steps.

"I say," Jasper said. "One wouldn't think Miss Lenox would go off and leave the job half-finished."

"It's probably a tricky thing," I said, "making sure someone is dead in a crevasse without joining them there."

"Quite. So back to the lounge, old bean? Looks to be another interesting chin-wag."

"Wouldn't miss it for the world."

CHAPTER 30

*M*r. Lavington insisted he was well enough to sit up. His leg was bound in a splint, so he was settled on the sofa with his leg propped up on a cushion. He also had a plaster on his forehead, and tiny cuts covered his hands. Swathed in blankets, which covered his torn and damp clothes, he looked like a war refugee. Vogel, perched on a chair to the right of Mr. Lavington, took out his notebook again. "You are a lucky man, Mr. Lavington. Few people survive the sort of fall you experienced. It's fortunate Mr. Blinkhorn and Mr. Hale heard your shouts."

"There was nothing lucky about it. I managed to catch hold of a tree root. It's only because I'm an experienced climber that I was able to hold on and then make my way up onto a small ledge."

"Indeed." Vogel paused while a hotel attendant put a glass of brandy down beside Mr. Lavington. After he'd had a long sip, Vogel continued, "I have a few questions. I'm sure you won't mind helping me clear up a few details.

Miss Juliet Lenox has shared some rather interesting information with us about you and your actions on the night your wife died."

Mr. Lavington put the drink down so carefully it didn't even make a noise when the crystal connected with the table. "I'm sure she has. I, however, have nothing to say to you without my solicitor."

"Of course," Vogel said in an agreeable tone. "But I should let you know Miss Lenox revealed your entire plan—how you duped Miss Lenox into helping you kill your wife. I must say it's quite reprehensible the way you took advantage of Miss Lenox. I can see why you wouldn't want to speak about it."

Mr. Lavington swiveled toward Vogel, cringed, then slowly turned his shoulders so that he was facing the korporale more fully. "That's completely wrong." He shook his head, and damp hair fell forward over the bandage on his forehead.

"But that's what she told us. Isn't it correct?" Vogel asked, pen poised, a look of confusion on his face.

"Yes, it's wrong. Utterly wrong." He reached for the brandy. "It was her idea—all of it. The blackmail note, getting Emmaline out of the way. Everything."

"Was it now?" Vogel asked with surprise in his voice.

Mr. Lavington pointed the brandy glass at Vogel. "She was the one who planned it. The whole thing—every bit of it. Juliet said the blackmail note was the perfect setup to get Emmaline onto the terrace and then we could take care of her there."

Vogel wrinkled his forehead into a doubtful expression. "But Miss Lenox was very distraught—weeping, in fact."

Mr. Lavington huffed. "That woman can cry at the drop of a hat. Believe me, I know. She planned everything down to the last detail. Juliet was the one who came up with the appointment on the terrace and the idea of catching her sleeve on fire to cover my exit. And she hid my ice axe in the trees near the wall so I'd have it to climb with and use on the terrace." His words were biting, his tone sharp. I exchanged a glance with Jasper, who widened his eyes and murmured in my ear, "Not quite the broken chap I spoke to the night his wife died."

I nodded my agreement. Mr. Lavington didn't look anything like the mourning, withdrawn creature Etta had described. He'd kept to his room and avoided interacting with people, which meant he only had to act the mourning widower in short bursts, like during his solitary visit to the dining room or on the trail with us in the forest.

"So we'll find Miss Lenox's fingerprints on the ice axe along with yours?" Vogel asked.

Mr. Lavington's gaze skittered right, then left. For a moment, it seemed he was contemplating springing up from the sofa and running, but he was boxed in with Vogel on one side and Jasper and I on the other. I think it was at that moment it dawned on him that he'd just admitted to a murder. He threw back the rest of the brandy and wiped his mouth with the back of his hand. "Yes, you will. I haven't removed it. Every time I went along there to pick it up, some blasted climber or skier or rambler came along." He sent Jasper and I a dirty look. "Juliet kept nagging me about it, so I told her I'd thrown it away in the forest."

"And where exactly did you leave it?"

"Check the tallest tree in the little copse on the left-hand side of the wall. There's a dead branch about five feet up. It's hooked over that. Juliet put it there before dinner that evening and . . . afterward, I replaced it before I returned to the hotel. I couldn't very well walk back into the lobby carrying an ice axe."

"Yes, that would have raised eyebrows," Vogel said mildly. "And you walked along the railing of the sun terrace to reach your wife so you wouldn't leave footprints going to her body. We know that." A stunned look traced across Mr. Lavington's face. Vogel, speaking as a father might with a child, said, "You might as well tell me the whole thing. Especially since your statement disagrees with Miss Lenox's. One of the two of you is lying. It may take a bit to work out who's telling fibs, but we will do it."

Mr. Lavington looked from Vogel to Jasper to me. Vogel gave me a small nod, and I said, "Oh, and I should let you know that I found the fabric that was used in Juliet's dress to keep it from burning her, and Mr. Rimington worked out the anagram for the room you reserved."

Mr. Lavington closed his eyes briefly as his head dipped forward. "I told Juliet that anagram was foolish, but she insisted. She thought it was amusing." He looked up, his shoulders still stooped over. "Now listen, I'm being straight with you, not like Juliet. She's lied through her teeth, and she'll keep on—in between crying bouts, of course. I'm cooperating with you. She's not."

Vogel said, "Noted. I appreciate your cooperation. I'll have to check your story, but if it's the truth, it will make a difference for you."

Mr. Lavington nodded. "Good. All right, then." He pushed his hair off his forehead with his left hand and leaned back against the cushions. "Juliet also insisted we stay here at Alpine House afterward and continue to avoid each other. We'd been keeping away from each other for months. We didn't want anyone to suspect we were together."

"No, I imagine not," Vogel said. "But you met secretly?"

"Yes, but only twice. Once on the train in the middle of the night, and today on the mountain. Juliet sent me a note. She said to slip out of the hotel, bring my skis, and meet her there."

"And this meeting on skis was not part of the plan?"

"No. Originally, I was to return to England for the funeral and stay there for a month before putting the word out that I was devastated and couldn't stay in the London house. I planned to put the house on the market and return to St. Moritz. That was the plan. We'd been over it again and again, so I was surprised she wanted to meet on the mountain today. When I arrived, there were no other skiers about except Juliet. It seemed to be safe, so I didn't avoid her." He stared at the empty fireplace for a moment, then continued, "By the time I realized what she intended, it was too late. I see now she'd maneuvered me into position right by the drop-off into the valley, exactly where she wanted me to be. She charged at me and shoved her pole into my shoulder."

He touched his upper arm gingerly. "I'll have a bruise there. I lost control and went over the edge. Fortunately, with all the fresh snow, it wasn't a terribly hard landing. As I said, I was able to grip a tree root to keep from falling to the bottom of the valley. She skied away after she shoved me, then circled back and waited at the top. I was tucked up under some bushes. I couldn't see her, but I could hear her breathing. She called my name a few times, but softly, as if she didn't want anyone else to hear her. I didn't answer."

"No, I imagine not," Vogel said.

"Juliet ran me off the mountain." He adjusted the position of the leg in the splint, grimacing as he moved. "She could have murdered me."

Vogel kept his eyes on his notepaper as he said, "Yes, there's a lot of that going around."

CHAPTER 31

The next morning Jasper and I went to the police station to sign our typed statements. We'd spent the previous day there, waiting to give our statements and then actually giving them to Oberwaller, who had written everything down in slow, careful notes.

Once we'd signed our statements, Jasper and I stood to leave, but Oberwaller said, "Wait here, please. Korporale Vogel wants to speak to you."

Vogel came from his office a moment later and said, "Let me walk you out," and escorted us into the late morning sunshine. "I thought you'd want to know we found the ice axe," he said as we went down the steps to the street. Workers were still clearing the fresh snow from the last storm off the street, piling it into the waist-high heaps that stretched down either side of the road.

"That quickly?" I asked.

"I sent an officer to look for it as soon as we took Lavington into custody. It was exactly where he said it

259

would be. Two sets of prints on it too. They match those of Miss Lenox and Mr. Lavington, which works out neatly, linking both of them to the crime." Vogel smoothed his Van Dyke beard and gave us a satisfied smile. "Mr. Lavington has been happy to provide more details about the asbestos fabric. He's rather anxious to make sure Miss Lenox doesn't get off. He's more than willing to expound on her involvement and keeps thinking of another detail to share."

"That works out well for you," I said.

"Yes, there is nothing better for a case than when a pair of criminals have a falling out. Lavington said during one of Miss Lenox's recent visits to London, a theater near her lodging was being fitted out with a new fire curtain. The old one was discarded. She saw it being removed and took some of it away to create the fireproof layer for the dress. It was the beginning of the plan they concocted—well," he amended, "the plan Miss Lenox concocted. According to Mr. Lavington, the initial idea and the plan were all hers. He simply executed it." Vogel winced. "Not the best choice of wording, I apologize."

"Sadly accurate, though," Jasper said.

"I mustn't keep you any longer," Vogel said, his tone turning brisk. "I hope the remainder of your stay in St. Moritz is pleasant."

"I shall be able to truly enjoy it now," I said.

"Good." He shook Jasper's hand. "Thank you, Mr. Rimington."

Jasper dipped his head. "Happy to pitch in, especially when it helps Olive."

Vogel turned to me. "Well done, Miss Belgrave. You are a—how do you say?—good fig?"

"Good egg," I amended with a smile.

"Yes, that's right. You're a good *egg*, Miss Belgrave. As are you, Mr. Rimington. And now I must return to my paperwork." Vogel said goodbye and returned to the police station.

As he opened the door, Mr. Blinkhorn came out. At least I thought it was Blinkhorn. He came down the steps and said hello to us. The dimple had made a fleeting appearance as Vogel shook his hand and waved him on his way. "Going back to the hotel, Mr. Blinkhorn?" I ventured.

I must have got it right because he didn't correct me and fell into step with us, crunching through the snow that remained on the road.

"Odd thing, to have to give a statement to the police during one's holiday, isn't it?" Blinkhorn said.

Jasper said, "Not really, no. I was expecting it, actually."

I playfully punched Jasper before linking arms with him. "Ignore Mr. Rimington. He often exaggerates," I said to Blinkhorn. "What did the police ask you?"

"They wanted to know how I knew Lavington. I wasn't much help to them. I only met him through the climbing club and had never had a conversation with him about anything but mountaineering. I must say it was dashed exciting," he added, "to be involved in a mountain rescue." But then his enthusiasm faded, and he looked across to the sawtooth line of the peaks on the other side of the valley. "But this news that Lavington is a murderer? I never would have thought he was that sort."

"No, one never does," I said, stepping over a slushy puddle.

Blinkhorn tilted his head in a questioning manner.

Jasper explained, "Murder follows Miss Belgrave, old thing. I'd watch out around her, if I were you."

Blinkhorn laughed—yes, the dimple was in evidence—so definitely Blinkhorn. But the sound was a bit forced, and as we arrived at the hotel, he sent me a sideways glance.

"As I said, best to ignore Mr. Rimington."

Blinkhorn made a noncommittal sound. "Sorry to run, but I must go. If all goes well, Hale and I have been invited to join a climb in the Himalayas. Must get in all the practice here that I can."

"Best of luck," I said.

He thanked us and hurried away.

"Skittish chap, isn't he?" Jasper paused so I could precede him into the hotel.

"You frightened him away."

"He'll get over it, I'm sure. And now we can discuss more personal things. I'm at your disposal. Do you have any plans for today? Perhaps a late breakfast to begin, then a perusal of snow globes later?"

"Sounds lovely."

We went to the rooftop restaurant and were seated near the railing on the side that overlooked the valley. The lake, a shining silvery-blue, reflected the snow-dusted hillsides, the outline of the peaks, and the cottony white clouds dotting the sky. Tiny figures of skaters glided and twirled on the frozen section of the lake. Farther out, skiers inched across the snow layer that covered the ice with smooth scissoring swings of their arms and legs.

The sun warmed my shoulders, and I removed my scarf and unbuttoned my coat. We gave our attention to enjoying the view and then to our breakfast. Eventually,

Jasper put down his coffee cup. "What else shall we do today?"

"You've finished your project?"

"I handed it off to Bebe this morning before we departed for the police station. Bebe will take it when she leaves with Mr. Vandenberg tomorrow." He squinted down at the ice rink closest to us. "They were on their way to skate. I suppose they're down there now."

"Probably skating in time with arms linked," I said.

"Most likely. They have that rosy halo of new love encircling them like a bubble."

"Do you think it will work out for them?" I asked, curious about his assessment of the pair. They seemed genuinely in love, but I didn't know Miss Ravenna as well as Jasper did.

"I should think so. Mr. Vandenberg is besotted, and I've never seen Bebe behave in such a manner. She's quite taken with him."

"That's good. I wonder where they'll live? It didn't sound as if they intended to return to Germany."

"No," Jasper said, "I don't think so. I wouldn't be surprised if they venture out to Hollywood."

"Now that could be interesting."

"Wouldn't it?"

I picked up the last slice of toast from the rack and buttered it. "Did I tell you I'm meeting Mrs. Ashford today? She offered to take me climbing. Would you like to come?"

"Sounds rather strenuous."

"I'm sure you'll be able to keep up. We must give it a go. When will we be in the Alps again?"

"There is that."

"I'm glad we have a few more days to enjoy our time here. What else would you like to do?"

"We must take a turn on the ice, I think."

"Yes, I agree. And I wouldn't mind giving skiing another go."

"You're an ambitious one, aren't you?"

A shadow fell over our table, and I looked up to find Hattie and Rob. I'd seen them on the other side of the restaurant, holding hands across the table. Jasper pushed back his chair and stood up. "Good morning. Would you like to join us?"

Hattie motioned him back into his seat. She wore a chic little toque with a fur-lined brim and a single ornamental flower on the crown that matched her traveling suit. "Oh no. Rob and I are on our way out. We wanted to stop for a moment to say goodbye and give you this." I took the business card Hattie held out to me. The address of the millinery was printed on it in raised letters. Under it, she'd written an address in St. Moritz and the note, *Fifty percent discount to be used at any time.* "I hope you'll stop by and have a look around. After all this with Juliet and Mr. Lavington—well! It's shocking, but to be perfectly honest, it's not *that* surprising. Juliet always was a schemer."

Rob didn't say anything, but the look on his face indicated he agreed.

"I know you were instrumental in sorting everything out," Hattie continued. "If you need a new hat for any of the press photographers, who I'm sure will track you down once the story breaks, do drop in. One of the boutiques here in town is now carrying some of my hats."

She sent a teasing look at her husband and patted his chest. "All those trucks and extra baggage fees were worth it."

"As usual, you were spot-on," Rob said, pride in his voice.

"Congratulations on the expansion." I tapped the card. "And thank you for this. I can always use a new hat."

Rob said, "Darling, we must go. We don't want to miss our train."

Jasper watched them make their way through the tables. "Well, they seem to be getting along well."

"Makes a change, doesn't it? Juliet said they enjoyed their little spats and that the blowups they had were temporary things."

"I suppose that's one way to conduct a marriage." Jasper wrinkled his nose. "Does sound rather fatiguing, though. I prefer a less fraught relationship."

"As do I."

"Well, that works out well, then. I'm glad we agree on that." He reached for my hand, and I wove my fingers through his. I must say, while the view was beautiful, my interest in it faded into the background.

We sat that way until the waiter arrived. I dropped my hands to my lap as he removed the plates and refilled Jasper's coffee. I reluctantly checked my watch. "We should go soon if we want time to visit the shops. I don't want to keep Mrs. Ashford waiting."

Jasper, who was looking over my shoulder, raised a hand. "There she is now. I believe she's looking for you."

I twisted around and spotted Mrs. Ashford moving with her confident tread through the tables to us. I reached for my handbag. "Am I late? I thought we were meeting in an hour and a half."

"Yes, you're correct, but I came to ask if you would mind delaying our climb until after luncheon."

"Not at all."

Jasper had stood to greet Mrs. Ashford, and now he pulled out a chair for her. "Thank you," she said as she took a seat. "I can only stay for a moment." She turned to me. "And thank you for your flexibility. I have a few things to take care of with the Ladies' Winter Sporting Association."

"I don't mind postponing until later. Mr. Rimington is interested in joining our little climbing expedition today."

Jasper added, "Do you have any objection to another novice?"

"None at all. You haven't climbed at all?" Mrs. Ashford asked.

"No, I've always managed to avoid it," he said with a straight face, but I knew him well enough to know he meant the reply to be humorous.

Mrs. Ashford looked as if she wasn't sure how to take the statement. "Well, I'm always delighted to introduce people to the sport."

"Such a lot of work, mountaineering, don't you know?" Jasper continued. "Now, tobogganing—that's a sport I can truly enjoy. Nothing to do but sit and lean one way or the other."

Mrs. Ashford, her tone shifting to the less-friendly end of the spectrum asked, "And are you hoping the club limits members to men only?"

"Good gad, no. Why? Someone banging on about that?"

"Unfortunately, yes." Mrs. Ashford frowned. "If it happens, we may have to create a separate women's tobogganing club, but hopefully we can stave that off." Mrs. Ashford turned to me. "Now, Miss Belgrave, the rumors are flying about. I think you have some insight to the situation. Do you foresee the police releasing Juliet?"

"I think that's extremely unlikely."

Mrs. Ashford drew in a breath. "Well. I suspected as much."

"Did you . . . ?"

"Have an idea about Juliet's involvement in Mrs. Lavington's death? No. But Juliet was very secretive about certain things—times when she was away and who she was meeting. I put it down to her being a modern girl who didn't want an old woman looking over her shoulder when it came to her men friends." Her voice lost its usual forceful cadence. "Appalling what happened," she said softly.

"What will happen with the association now that Juliet is—er—"

"No longer part of it?" Mrs. Ashford asked. "It will go on, of course. It may be a bit bumpy for a while. My inability to completely see Juliet's true nature has left me in the lurch. I have some details to take care of before tomorrow's ladies' race—that's why I can't meet you until this afternoon—and I'll certainly need a new secretary, but that can be sorted out quickly."

"So the race will go on?" I asked.

"Undoubtedly. The world of sport provides many important functions, such as allowing us an escape from all the unpleasantness in the world—politics, personalities, even crime—if only for the length of a race." She switched her attention to Jasper as she added, "And it provides an opportunity to challenge oneself, which is always a good thing."

He held up a hand as if to ward off her glare. "I agree, in theory. In practice, I'd rather read a book."

Mrs. Ashford let out a sharp laugh. "I'm fond of a good novel myself, so I can't fault you there." She picked up her handbag. "I must go. I'll handle a few minor details for the race, and then I'll introduce you to the *best* alpine sport: mountaineering." She stabbed a finger on the table to emphasize her statement.

"We look forward to it," I said, and then we agreed to meet in the lobby at one o'clock. She strode away, nearly taking out a slow-moving waiter who barely dodged out of her path.

Jasper asked, "Was that a threat?"

"You'd better enjoy mountaineering—or else!" We laughed, and then I said, "I'm sure we'll have a wonderful time. She's just—passionate."

"If you say so, old bean. What should we do after the climb?"

"I'm sure *collapse* will be at the top of my list."

A hotel attendant approached our table. "A telephone call has come through for you, Miss Belgrave."

"A telephone call? Who could be so extravagant as to call me?"

Jasper said he'd take care of our bill. I jumped up and did a good impression of Mrs. Ashford's parting-the-crowd stride. International telephone rates were rather dear, so I didn't want to waste a minute more than was necessary. The attendant took me to Mr. Hoffman's empty office.

I picked up the receiver from the desk and leaned in nearer the mouthpiece. "Hello?"

A few crackles followed, and then a woman's voice came through the line. "Olive? It's Minerva."

"What's wrong? What's happened?" I'd expected to hear my father or Gwen on the line, not my friend who lived in the flat across from mine.

"Nothing terrible—at least nothing that I know of," she said quickly through the static. "Evans has been holding your post as you asked, but you have a letter here labeled *urgent*. He asked me what I thought we should do about it. The word is written on the envelope in all capitals and underlined twice. There's no return address. I thought perhaps I should open it, but I didn't like to do so without consulting you. A telephone call, while extravagant, seemed the most expeditious way of reaching you."

"Yes, please open it," I said, conscious of the very expensive seconds ticking away, like my heart, which was beating quicker than normal. Urgent mail, like unexpected telegrams, rarely brought good news.

"All right, let's see. It says, 'Dear Miss Belgrave, I have heard of your talents and think that you might be just the person to help me with a little problem. A mutual friend informs me that you're traveling in Switzerland now, and I hope this missive is forwarded to you in time to reach you before you return to England. If it does, you would be most welcome to visit me at my home and stay with me for a few days while I explain everything. I hope to meet you soon. Sincerely, Lucy Twissel.'"

"How odd," I said, relief washing through me that the urgent news was nothing to do with my family or friends.

"There's an address in France under her name,"

Minerva said. "Well, I'm sorry I rang you. That's not quite what I thought it would be. I imagined it was something truly ghastly, like a death in the family or something of that nature."

"Yes, I thought the same thing. Let me get some paper —" I found a blank sheet of typing paper and picked up a pencil. "I'm ready now. Read it to me again, and I'll jot it down."

Minerva repeated it, and I wished I'd been working on shorthand instead of touch-typing. Then Minerva said, "I'll send you a telegram if I receive anything else from this Lucy."

"Yes, do. Jasper and I are here for a few more days. But I may divert and meet Lucy Twissel on my way home. It might take a few more days."

"No problem at all. Your postmistress remains on the job."

I hung up and met Jasper in the lobby. "What's happened, Olive? Is it your father?"

"No, nothing like that. Everyone at home is fine." I explained why Minerva had telephoned and said, "The letter was from a stranger. She found out through a mutual acquaintance I'm in Switzerland and invited me to visit her. She wants my help to solve a *little problem*, as she phrased it, before I return to England. No details."

"Hmm . . . little problems are rarely labeled urgent."

"Yes, I agree. It's from a Lucy Twissel."

Jasper had been taking a cigarette out of his case, but his head popped up at the name. "Lucy Twissel? Are you sure?"

"The connection wasn't wonderful, but I was able to

hear Minerva fairly well, and she repeated the name twice."

"Well then, I better come along too."

"Why?"

"Because Lucy Twissel is my aunt."

Sign up for Sara's updates to get exclusive content and early looks at the books at SaraRosett.com/signup.

THE STORY BEHIND THE STORY

Thank you for joining Olive on her first international case. I like writing about the 1920s, but researching this book was especially enjoyable because it let me delve into the high society winter playground of St. Moritz and the birth of winter sports.

The mountains have always been a favorite vacation destination for me, beginning with the summer trips to the Rocky Mountains my family took when I young, a tradition my husband and I carried on with our family. In fact, I began writing *Murder in the Alps* in an alpine setting during a recent vacation, although it was Colorado instead of Switzerland. I haven't been able to travel to St. Moritz itself, except through my research. However, I did make a road trip through the Alps from Germany to Venice, which inspired a book in my On the Run series, *Suspicious*. The views were spectacular, and our meandering journey included visits to Garmisch-Partenkirchen, where we went to the top of the Zugspitze (via cable car, not climbing!) as well as the hike to the ruin of Ehrenberg Castle in Austria.

I enjoy searching for interesting facts about the 1920s, but learning about the police force in Switzerland in 1924 was a challenge. Thankfully, Sandra Nay of the Graubünden State Archives and Anita Senti, Head of Communications of the Cantonal Police, came to my rescue. Thanks, too, to Alexander Rechsteiner of the Swiss National Museum for taking the time to help me find the people who could answer my questions. *Danka!*

Both men and women enjoyed competing on the Cresta Run from its beginning in the late 1800s. According to the *Online Skeleton Scrapbook* (https://www.sven-holger.com/en/online-skeleton-scrapbook/), Mrs. J. M. Baguley was the last woman to win a race on the course in 1925, but women continued to toboggan on the Cresta until 1929, when they were banned by the St. Moritz Tobogganing Club because of "health concerns." In 2018, women were welcomed back into the club and can now ride the Cresta.

The character of Mrs. Ashford was based on the accounts I read about the early women climbers. If you're interested in learning more about female "alpists," I recommend *Mountaineering Women: Stories by Early Climbers* by David Mazel. An internet search will also turn up some amazing photos of women in long skirts marching up ice steps and crossing crevasses on ladders— quite a sight!

Olive will be back with another case, but I'm taking a break to work on *Murder Among the Pyramids*, the first book in a new series, the High Society Lady Traveler series. It's a spin-off from the High Society Lady Detective series and is also set in the 1920s.

If you enjoy the Olive books, you'll also like *Murder Among the Pyramids*. And don't worry! I have many more Olive books planned.

If you'd like a note when my next book is coming out, please sign up for my updates at SaraRosett.com/signup. You'll also get my personal mystery book recommendations as well as exclusive content and giveaways.

ALSO BY SARA ROSETT

This is Sara Rosett's complete library at the time of publication, but Sara has new books coming out all the time. Sign up for her Notes and News Updates at SaraRosett.com/signup to get exclusive content and information on new releases.

Available in Ebook, Audio, and Print

High Society Lady Detective

Murder at Archly Manor

Murder at Blackburn Hall

The Egyptian Antiquities Murder

Murder in Black Tie

An Old Money Murder in Mayfair

Murder on a Midnight Clear

Murder at the Mansions

Murder in the Alps

Coming soon

High Society Lady Traveler

Murder Among the Pyramids

Murder on Location

Death in the English Countryside

Death in an English Cottage

Death in a Stately Home

Death in an Elegant City

Menace at the Christmas Market (novella)

Death in an English Garden

Death at an English Wedding

On the Run

Elusive

Secretive

Deceptive

Suspicious

Devious

Treacherous

Duplicity

Non-fiction

The Bookish Sleuth: A Mystery Reader's Journal and Calendar

How to Write a Series

How to Outline a Cozy Mystery

Made in the USA
Columbia, SC
28 December 2024

50794214R00169